BIRMI...
Univers...

Borderlands

AN ANTHOLOGY

Edited by
**Suna Afshan, Laurie Calcutt, Charlotte McCormac,
Holly Louise Psaliou and Naush Sabah**

Published by twentyfivefiftytwo
for and on behalf of The School of English,
Birmingham City University.

First published 2019
Compilation © The School of English,
Birmingham City University 2019
Contributions © individual copyright holders

This is a work of fiction. Any views, opinions or statements expressed in
this work are those of the individual authors and not the Publisher.

A CIP Catalogue record for this book is available
from the British library

ISBN 978-1-9996653-6-4

Designed and typeset by Mark Bracey

Printed and bound by CPI Group (UK) Ltd, Croydon, CR0 4YY

Contents

Foreword

Amanda Smyth

Borderlands. I was struck here by the rich quality of work. I had never thought of borders in so many ways. But here we have a variety of deeply affecting pieces forcing the reader to really look at how borderlands exist in our world.

In this fine collection, we are reminded of the terrifying border between life and death when a narrator experiences a stroke and her life is forever changed. The passage between old and new, a past life and the next, leaving an old self behind while trying to glimpse a future. There is the borderland of sickness/wellness populated by nurses and machines. There are geographical borders, travelling from city to countryside: new territory crossed into easily by hopping over a stream. There are poems about migration and the pain of leaving lands and people behind. Stories and poems about artificial borders erected within the countries of our hearts; psychological borders put there to protect ourselves from damage. Reading this work, I was reminded of how, in order to grow and move into new territory, we must cross borders within ourselves. Sometimes it is frightening and it can be liberating. It requires courage.

For some writers here, this might be the first time they are seeing their work in print. Some will make the decision to become writers, and others may leave it behind. My own writing mentor once told me, writing will not make you rich, but it will make your life rich. I knew that it would be a hard and long and difficult road. I can assure you it doesn't get any easier. But once you cross over into a place—within yourself—where writing is more than just a hobby, when you commit fully and wholly to the writing, then things begin to change and move. There are many gifts.

The journey isn't smooth; there are many dangerous borders to cross. For some, it may look less difficult. It is easy to compare your own journey with another. To compare your journey or your work with others is a pointless occupation — a distraction. Just as it is pointless to compare countries, bodies, skin, houses, flowers. Your work is *your* work, and it speaks to you and answers you in every moment. If you do it, it will give you back all you give. If you ignore it, it will look back at you with its hands in its pockets.

When I first saw my work in print, I was inspired to keep going. I hope that will be the case for all the contributing authors here.

No Dreams of This Place
Suna Afshan

We've lived in this semi-detached for seven years now,
painted the doors and bannisters each spring.
Settees we bought on the Alum Rock Road,
charcoal grey with massive magenta lilies,
were all the rage then, but are erring on kitsch now.
The wardrobes, the beds, and the mattresses we bought
together from a shop on a hill somewhere in Small Heath,
and we sit comfortably, our cricket team of a family,
on the cracking burgundy leather sofas in the lounge.
And all this is to say, that every knick-knack on the mantle,
every framed photo of wedding, birthday, or even that one
where three sisters sit on a barrier of the M6 hard shoulder
dressed in plaid pinafores, velvet headbands and bob cuts,
are efforts to breathe a little bit of home into this house.
We've hung up our moth-bitten underwear on the line,
carved initials into the bark of an unfurling evergreen,
we've erected snowmen with mud-acne and ice-tumours
(this spring, one stood like a scarecrow in front of the shed,
and when it melted all that was left was his Lego face).
Yet, two nights ago over a habitual cup of ten o'clock tea,
I turned to my brother and said, 'No dreams of this place.
Tonight, even, I dreamt of the Wright Road house,
and I was crawling on the upstairs landing like a soldier.
Remember how that tiny garden wasn't always paved,
and when it was we played that game of human checkers?
How we made skipping ropes from PlayStation controllers?
In the summer holidays we skipped for hours on that rug outside.

I still remember the way it burned my feet.'
Today, looking up, while I painted the kitchen's skirting,
seeing the pink plaster seam of this new extension
beside the layers of wallpaper the O'Connells had left us with,
all homage to woodland caricatures and seventies bold-print,
a flash of bold script on the faded paper beneath it
   caught my eye:
MELISSA WAS HERE AND SO WAS JONATHON — 19/04/59

City's Edge

Chris Fewings

You're upstairs on the No. 50 bus in Kings Heath High Street. The traffic always clogs here, as people flock to shops supplied by juggernauts with goods funnelled in from around the world: money pours into the tills. Outside a supermarket, a child's bike chained to a lamp post serves as a blue plaque: Hope, aged 13, was killed right here by a distracted lorry driver.

If time froze on the bus, yet the buildings all around it vanished, taking you back a couple of centuries, you'd see how the land falls gently to the west towards a little river they call the Rea. Over your right shoulder is the brook that sculpted Highbury Park running down towards the river. To the east – your left – instead of the redbrick Methodist church at the top of Cambridge Road, you might spot the source of Coldbath Brook, which falls through Moseley Bog to Sarehole millpool and the River Cole – places where Tolkien and his brother played as children when their rented house, three miles from the centre, stood at the edge of the rapidly growing city.

This ancient track (now the A435) became a turnpike road in the 18th century, a toll road, connecting Worcestershire farms to the small but growing town of Birmingham to the north. You see the heathland on either side that isn't worth cultivating. Time outside the bus moves forward. The road improves, and fields appear around you as demand in Birmingham swells. The railway cuts deeply through the land in 1840; new buildings appear along what has become a high street; the suburb's population explodes as Birmingham expands – the city swallows Kings Heath whole in 1911.

The present reasserts itself; the traffic moves. The bus stops at a crossroads in a hollow. The only stream you can see here now is made up of half-ton chunks of metal and plastic growling at the traffic lights, belching invisible soot, carbon and nitrous oxides, drinking petroleum and gulping oxygen.

The lights turn green. It's late spring: even the tallest of the street trees are in full leaf. You're in the northern part of Shakespeare's Arden Forest, which in his time was a patchwork of woods and ploughland and pasture and unruly hedges stretching to Stratford. Trees have been cleared in the centuries since to grow grain and cattle, to provide firewood for the hearth, to make charcoal to smelt iron, to build tea clippers and Nelson's navy, to accommodate hedgerow-hating tractors, and to make way for acre after acre of houses, shops and factories, schools, hospitals and churches. You're glad of your front seat. The leaves brushing the glass lift your spirits.

Soon, a steep hill down to a canal. You see the sports centre on your left, but not the little wood tucked behind it. You don't notice the Chinn Brook alongside the canal at the bottom of the valley: it runs into the Cole by Trittiford Pool, where the mill had four stones for grinding corn in 1783. You don't realise that on your right the Chinn now boasts a tiny local nature reserve (they call it Jasmin Fields, but much of it is dense scrubby woodland).

The bus climbs up the other side. Onto the Maypole, a whirligig of traffic connecting the city to the motorway beyond. You turn sharp right. A dozen thirteen-storey blocks rise around you, surrounded by prefabricated terraced houses. Slum clearances in the 1960s spawned estates of council housing on the city circumference, wherever land was cheap. When the bus drops downhill and stops in the valley bottom you look left and notice a line of trees leading to a row of prefabs. You guess the trees grew by a stream which now runs underground. You alight and follow them.

A sign by a footpath: Walkers Heath Park. You enter. Here's the stream, not much bigger than a ditch, but graced with trees and rocky interruptions – when you look at a map at home you'll find out this is Chinn Brook, and follow its course with your finger to the River Cole. You're surprised how big the park is as you wander round broad mown paths cut through long grass. The hedges are filled with hawthorn flower and blossoming rowan trees abound: two shades of glorious white in the late May evening sunshine which has finally emerged from the clouds to welcome you. Over the stream, up a bridleway: a hayfield on your left, a grazed field on your right. Are you still in Birmingham? Perhaps you've crossed the border into Worcestershire.

Back to the stream to seek its source. Along a track, across a narrow road, into some very rough pasture. You scramble down to the stream itself and find a muddy path. Soon, you're blocked by barbed wire. Back through the park, past ball courts, playground and allotments to another bus stop. From the top deck, you notice more partly wooded open space on the other side of the road, surrounded by what you guess is social housing. In a few weeks you'll return, following the brook downstream in that direction, and find clumps of mixed native woodland; a surprising line of pines on the brook's bank; the torso of a rusty burnt-out motorbike asking to be photographed: an accidental work of art. Then unmanicured scrubland will lead to a canal – must be the same one the bus crossed over – and you'll see the stream tunnel under it. It'll be drizzling, none too warm. You'll feel like an explorer, absurdly pleased to find this place, to belong to this city of surprises.

EU Twenty Seven

Max Mulgrew

I have finally visited all the countries that are not planning to leave the European Union.

Every particle of light had been swallowed by clouds, the stone walls, the slate roof, the green shutters. The generator had stopped. I was eleven years old and alone in a black room of iron bedsteads, horsehair mattresses and scratchy woollen blankets. I woke up needing a wee. I was terrified of the naked wooden floor. When the lights were on, I had caught sight of silverfish and scuttling cockroaches. Now I imagined a mass of insects being crushed under my feet as I felt my way along the wall to the stairs and down to the door. When I got outside, I could hear waves beating the rocks in the cove. I detected a melancholy hint of dawn as I relieved myself on the turf. I ignored the blowback as the wind wafted from the sea.

This was Brittany in 1964. I was on a backpacking trip with my mother. We had arrived on Île de Batz by fishing boat in a storm. The only accommodation was in the *auberge de jeunesse* and we were the only guests. Rural France then was a country of quirky cars, trains that picked up farmers in fields, labourers wearing *bleu de travail*, squat toilets and garlic. Pigs roamed in the woods and children collected snails along drainage ditches. I loved it and the trip triggered an urge to travel.

***

When I was eighteen, I hitchhiked to Greece. That was a list-maker's dream. I visited Belgium, Luxembourg, West Germany,

Austria, Yugoslavia and Italy. Over the years, I ticked off many more countries. I admit I like making mental lists. They help to bring closure when they are completed, and they help to bring sleep. Try naming all fifty US states as you lie in bed and you will be drifting off in Mississippi. Compile an alphabetical list, one for each letter, of rivers and you will be getting zeds long before you reach the Zambezi. My compulsion to visit every country in Europe, then list them in my mind, was starting to keep me awake. How could I get to all the newly independent nations that emerged from the break-ups of the Soviet Union, Yugoslavia and the Eastern Bloc? How do you even define Europe?

I watched TV as the results of the June 26, 2016 Brexit referendum came in from Sunderland to Bridgend, Boston to Sandwell. I had been blithely crossing borders in the European Union for years. Suddenly the UK had voted to leave. I thought of the twenty-seven countries that would remain in the EU. It made me recall cycling in Amsterdam, cross-country skiing in Sweden, canyoneering in Spain, finding Heidegger's hideaway in the Black Forest and Tito's hideaway on the island of Vis in Croatia. Despite the smug reminiscences I was surprised at how many of the EU remainers I had not been to – the Baltic states, Poland, Czech Republic, Slovakia, Hungary, Romania, Bulgaria, Slovenia and tiny Malta. Now I had a simple list to complete. I decided a country visit must involve walking the streets, eating a meal and staying for at least one night. I became an expert at finding cheap flights from Birmingham, to fit in with days off work.

***

The challenge started with a £25 one-way flight to Bucharest and little idea how to get home again. I walked in 40°C heat to see 'Ceausescu's palace', the vast government building built before the dictator was shot. I had a cold beer from a kiosk in a park and I ate grilled meat in the old town. I had a good feeling. That night I found a flight back to the UK from Sofia. That would enable me to tick off another country and get home to Birmingham for £30. The train creaked slowly out of Bucharest at the start of the thirteen-hour journey. The locomotive looked as though it had been hit by shrapnel, the compartments were sweltering and the windows barely opened. We crept through vast fields of corn, wheat and sunflowers.

Just north of the Danube, we stopped at a village station. Officials boarded the train and took everyone's passports and identity cards away. Across an orchard, I could see a road checkpoint. Queues of lorries and cars had backed up. We were about to leave one EU nation and enter another, but this was definitely a hard border. Eventually passports were returned and the train rattled across a bridge over the expanse of the Danube. At the first station in Bulgaria it squealed to a halt and Bulgarian border officials came to take our documents away again. I finished my bottled water as we waited in the boiling heat for another thirty minutes.

It made me recall other difficult border crossings – being stuck on a similar train between Yugoslavia and Greece, having to walk across 'no man's land' between Malaysia and Thailand, facing a US immigration interrogation after a flight to Pittsburgh, being stopped at gunpoint by a UDA patrol during the Troubles and being told 'no' when I tried to join a Finnish boat trip into Russia.

***

I got a one-way ticket again, this time to Lithuania, and nearly missed the connecting flight in Brussels. I sprinted through the airport thinking, 'I do not want a night in Brussels. I've done that before.' I got to the plane just as they were about to close the doors. My list was critical – it was Vilnius or bust. I had a meal sitting cross-legged in a vegan 'yoga restaurant', explored the old city and wandered around grand squares and boulevards, then visited Vilnius's self-declared independent republic of Užupis – a hippy quarter where part of the constitution states,

'People have the right to be happy.' There was no problem at the Užupis border.

There was a cheap seat on a flight to Tallinn and I left Vilnius airport on a small turboprop. It was winter, but the sun was shining. We crossed the Estonian border and entered a blinding snowstorm. The propellers whipped the flakes into a frenzy as the plane lurched towards my next destination. A tram was waiting at Tallinn airport's doors ready to push through the drifts on its way into the city. Miniature snow ploughs were clearing the pavements as I marched down towards the harbour. Children wearing hats, mitts and boots were playing outside a school. I looked out across the frozen Baltic Sea towards Helsinki, in the EU's northernmost state.

***

As I arrived at work after time off between shifts, colleagues would ask, 'Where have you been this time?' 'Riga. It's a brilliant place.' 'Only Prague.' 'In a Budapest bathhouse.' Eventually they stopped asking. I ate cheesy potato dumplings in Bratislava; in Valetta, I joined government workers buying pastizzi, and in Krakow, my pierogi were filled with cabbage and wild mushrooms. Another day, another dumpling.

Now I was about to complete the list. On my teenage hitch-hiking trip to Greece I had slept in forests, on parched scrubland where shepherds and their flocks passed in the night, on beaches, next to roads, and on a bench in the grounds of Ljubljana castle. Slovenia was then part of Yugoslavia - I felt it needed a fresh visit as a full EU member. Number twenty-seven.

Mount Triglav is a fierce rocky peak in the Julian Alps and is the highest mountain in the country. All true Slovenes must climb Triglav, I was told. I joined them, as a true European, and every hiker greeted me with a friendly 'Dobre dan'. Hundreds of people equipped with helmets and safety harnesses were making for the top. It is an arduous trek and most climbers stay in mountain huts such as Planika, 2,400 metres above sea level. I do not know whether it was the altitude or the beer being drunk during the evening that caused the men and women in the dormitory to snore so loudly, but it made me feel wistful about the quiet of that Breton hostel on Île de Batz. I needed to get up in the night, although this time there were no cockroaches to worry about. I crept outside. There was a chemical toilet well away from the building, across jagged rocks. I had nothing on my feet, so I decided to take a risk with the chilly wind howling round the mountain. The moon lit up the crags and pinnacles. I thought I could see climbers' headlamps on the ridge leading to the summit. I was in love with Europe.

Mud Person

Suna Afshan

With mango skin, and mango flesh, and mango heart gone,
the only lasting memento this makeshift children's oven.

Muddled clay and straw and well water made their homes,
and in the sore summer they baked in cardboard cartons.

Two weeks for the crockery to morph into earthenware,
each saucer embroidered with fingerprints and sebum,

the eyes and nose and mouths gouged out by uneven nails,
dolls in my mother's palm, adorned with hay and stones.

With her godliness she forged life crudely from the earth,
turned the box on its side, and it became their kitchen.

She taught them to cook stews of stolen rice and carcass,
and fed their children: two knuckles wide and three long.

And they fell asleep to lullabies in my mother's tongue,
a tuck so tight, they were limbless dirt come morning.

The Bog Mirror
Suna Afshan

A feral crow aimed its arrowed bill
at a swollen corpse suspended
and still between the jade curd.

A packet of prawn cocktail crisps
swam in the sprawling reeds,
uglier in its half-life than any dead thing.

I came here with a poorly reflection:
it rippled in the pith of every eye,
the thing an echo, a little of me dubbed.

And I lay here with the rotten daffodils
on the banks of the bog-mirror to watch
my petulant shadow stay standing,
watch her lift her arms gently skyward,
and spin in place like some godless dervish.

Nobody

Chris Fewings

A light glows in a bedroom window, late.
Inside, a young man crumples up an email:
the party (or his invitation)'s cancelled.
He sniffs round Facebook, fires off messages
and comments. No replies. He waits five minutes.
Nothing. Four more minutes. Not a squeak.
The flat upstairs is silent. The street's empty.

He tries his answerphone: no messages.
He phones a friend and hears a hollow laugh;
gets scissors; cuts the phone line. He climbs the chimney -
stands there demanding gifts from passing reindeer
training for next week. The sleighs are empty.
A sudden snowstorm knocks him to the street

then blows away. He tries to thumb a lift:
no dice. The pub's a walk away: it slams
its doors as he arrives. The hiss of air
he liberates from parked tyres sounds human;
he remembers the long sighs when she

still slept beside him. Wanting to confess,
he tries to wave down a police car. It just
speeds up as it passes. He contemplates
the gutter as he sits down on the kerb:

no leaves or litter. A snow blanket would
seem a comfort now, but every flake
has melted. His story's soaking into tarmac.

He checks for missing persons. He's not listed.
He checks his pulse. A murmur. He murmurs back

and falls into a nightmare, where he bids

for boxing gloves on eBay. They arrive
by 3D printer instantly. His fist

goes through the screen, grabs a paper: a threat
in screaming capitals. He throws his gauntlets
down. The screen transforms into a mask

of Munch's *Scream*'s yelling at him. Perhaps
this is the only gift he'll get, unwrapped.
He grabs it quick, and pulls it on, and finds
a gallery; strolls in like an actor

and lifts a portrait off the wall, Norwegian.
He prints a copy off in oils: the hands
around the face snatch a knife and slash
the canvas. The cops are on his tail, but when
they question him remotely won't believe

he's guilty: no prison cell will touch him. The window
of the nightmare's triple glazed and curtained:
no one hears him howl. The walls are padded:
no echo answers him. The room is shrinking
round him. His body fades; his hands, detached,
type this on the keyboard – one stanza still...

No Soup

Adrian B. Earle

The darkness beyond the threshold is complete. It breathes.

A slab of nothingness where a cupboard used to be. Not a can or carton to be found. She reaches left into the murk for the light switch she knows is on the wall at shoulder height, only to feel her fingers curl around the pillar of the frame into that nothingness. She notices it is cool and slightly damp. She notices in that same long second, that the floor has absented itself.

The usual olive cracked linoleum, the single sheet that had somehow gone the twenty years since the flat's construction without being adhered to the concrete, is gone. She doesn't miss it. It stank of stale cigarette smoke. It reeked thanks to the previous occupiers. The fug of it seeped upwards after every spring clean. By June each year, the end of each sleeve and the dangling ends of every scarf were steeped in the stench of cheap cigarillos. She is glad that it's gone, she allows the gladness to ramble over the quietly insistent question of where the offending floor covering could have disappeared to. She wouldn't have minded the sudden disappearance of the shitty lino, if not for the fact that the concrete floor beneath is also gone. Gone in a way that made the decision of where to stand rather complicated.

Shuffling to the doorframe, she plants her feet on the pine flooring of the hallway and leans as far into the dark as she dares. The thin bronze strip of a draught excluder is now a precipice. She sees nothing beyond the boundary but feels the dark extend. She feels it in the way a rodent senses the opening of space above her mousy head. Knows the vastness of human habitat once she leaves the confines of her tunnel through the skirting. She feels the vast cavern of air extending up above her despite her inability to see the ceiling.

She is sure the void in place of her pantry has dimensions, boundaries. It must have. Everything has. But those dimensions, where the dark begins and where it ends, such geometry is outside of her current capabilities. All she wants is soup. She is already warming the bread under the grill. Just a little to crisp the crust the way she likes it. Heated to better receive the butter.

Barefoot, with her toes touching the rapidly cooling metal of the draft exclusion strip, she waves her hand through the dense, cool dark. She considers in that moment that the flat is nothing but an antechamber. A dull domestic entrance room built to proceed into whatever this space is.

Stepping back into the hallway, she closes the door, carefully folding the overstocked coat hook on the back of the door so as not to trap a sleeve in the jamb. She assumes there must be some mistake, that she used the door incorrectly. Perhaps turned that handle in some way she hadn't considered before. Maybe she has broken the room? She wonders if it is possible to break an entire room. She concludes after more moments staring at the door to nothingness that all things can break.

She is aware that rooms disappearing are not normal occurrences. She has lived 28 years without a single incident of a vanishing room. Vanishing objects within rooms. But not entire rooms. She considers whether a pantry can be called a room. She wonders if having a pantry made her and Graham posh? Noting that if so, they no longer had to worry about the burden of their privilege. It does not make her feel any better. Any darkness behind a closed door had never gone so far as to swallow the walls and floor. She wonders whether that is something she should be thankful for. She wonders about the sensation of the room disappearing while she is inside.

Retreating to the living room. Still hungry but the idle craving for soup, or maybe pasta is buried under the growing fear that the nothingness behind the door might spread. She fears the hallway wouldn't be safe. She fears that nowhere is safe. To leave the flat would mean walking past the yawning dark. Coats and gloss-painted plywood would be little protection. Then there was the front door itself.

The front door was newly fitted, solid oak, impermeable. She hated the new door. She hated it because Graham had called the fitters to put it in when she was out. She had come home to an alien front door. Her home was no longer her home. The new door had been installed without the glass panes that the older door had. The older door had glass panes reaching from the middle bar of the letterbox to the arch of the frame. This door stood solid, resolute, without a trace, no single reminder that a world lay on the other side of it.

Graham wanted them to change the design. Graham said the frosted glass was a 'glaring security risk'. She liked the glass. It meant that in the case of visitors she could see the person on the other side of the door. Discern the familiar shape of a takeaway delivery guy from that of a murderer. She wonders what a murderer would look like through frosted glass.

The new door has no glass. No way to see what exists beyond its threshold. She considers for a moment that if she opened the door to escape the dark only to find more darkness, what would she do? She had no idea that the pantry had absented itself when she'd opened the door. Maybe, she thinks, maybe the hallway outside the flat is also gone and she doesn't know.

Suddenly cold, she curls her legs underneath her. She wants to talk to somebody, anybody. She reaches for the phone but finds herself unable to dial. The numbers and names are less of a problem than what she could possibly say.

'Morning, Mum.'

'I'm fine. Good. Yeah.'

'Haven't eaten yet, no.'

'Why? Oh nothing. Just the pantry. Is gone.'

Graham wouldn't be any more receptive. He was always quick to tell her she was being irrational. For Graham every problem was caused by her being emotional. She hated it when he called her 'silly'. When he came home three hours late without answering his phone she was 'over-reacting'. When he says he will handle dinner and she comes home to him playing computer games, her frustration is 'further complicating the situation'. He never outright called her crazy, she knew he didn't need to. Just the thought of trying to explain the void in the pantry to him made her feel crazy. She thinks for the first time in a long time maybe she is mad. Maybe this is what it feels like to lose your mind. She doesn't feel crazy. But, she thinks, maybe that is just how these things work.

The ligaments in her knees begin to set. The skin on her legs is bloodless from the compression. Cold as a corpse. Cold and stubbled as granddad's cheek; she remembers being held up to kiss him in his coffin. She was embarrassed as she rose that he would see under the frills of her dress. She really had meant to shave her legs. It's funny how you remember these things. She had only been four when he stopped living. She didn't know the point at which she could only remember him dead.

The acrid taint on the air meant her toast was burning. She felt it grow in volume until it tickled at the corners of her eyes and the back of her throat. She cannot shake the image of the dark behind the door. It roars, a deep rumble that drowns out the tinny wail of the smoke alarm. She wonders what would be worse, burning to death or falling through infinite nothing for eternity.

*****

There must have been keys in the door, a familiar rattle and shuffle of his entrance. She hears instead:

'Fuck's sake, babe!' Anger makes his voice high and rasping. A sort of frustrated whine. 'Trying to fucking kill yourself! Are you fucking mad? look at it.' He must be in the kitchen now, 'It's fucking charcoal. How could you be so careless?'

'Hello to you too darling. How was your day?' she replies. 'The void has come to take us,' she thinks. She says, 'No really, I'm fine.'

She is undecided as to whether she is more insulted by the accusation of carelessness or the inane suggestion anyone would deliberately kill herself through the burning of toast. She uncurls from the sofa and stands stretching the feeling back into her legs as Graham thunders about opening windows and wafting smoke.

'Are you *trying* to burn the flat down...eh? With your bloody toast?'

'I forgot, I was sort of dealing with...'

'With what? Straightening your hair or something? You can't just start cooking and forget it, Meghan. We've talked about this.'

'When have we "talked about this" Graham?'

Another knife in his arsenal, every problem he had with her was endemic however small.

'You do this all the time, for fuck's sake.'

His usual reply. 'You forget things, you're careless.'

She decides, upon consideration that burning to death would be preferable to infinite falling through space.

She reasons, eventually, that the intense heat would crisp all nerve endings to the point of unresponsiveness. After all, piles of charred bone feel nothing. Falling, on the other hand, was never lethal. It was the stopping at the end that got you. Falling without end, she decided, was just another way of starving to death then desiccating in the cold emptiness at the end of all things. She wasn't about that.

She wonders if she had concluded earlier that a fiery end was better than an endless descent into the dark, she would have stayed with Graham after the work party. Whether she would have pressed on instead of folding when she confronted him about his work 'friend'. If she would have accepted the: 'placing-my-hand-on-the-arse-of-Claire-from-marketing-during-half-an-hour-of-conversation-that-was-really-just-five-minutes-you-are-massively-exaggerating-and-no-people-didn't-know-you-were-my-girlfriend-because-YOU-didn't-introduce-yourself-and-besides-we-are-close-it's-just-what-friends-do-and-you'd-know-if-you-had-any-male-friends' excuse he machine-gunned at her until she fell silent. Better to explode than fade she thinks.

Graham is still wafting and swearing, she wonders why Graham can't take his wafting and swearing nearer to the actual smoke alarm that is still wailing. Its strangled meeps piercing even the cold stillness of her torpor. She wishes the alarm would go away. She wishes Graham with his stomping and his swearing and his judgment would just go away. She wishes she wasn't even here. She considers for a single tick of her watch that she in fact isn't here. That she, Megan, has left somehow, probably without letting herself know she was going out. That feeling is further compounded by Graham storming past to open yet another window, concentrating the cold without paying her the slightest mind.

He doesn't see me, she thinks. But then again, he's never seen her. Because she is now invisible, she decides she should also remain silent. She thinks it only appropriate for those who go unseen to also go unheard.

So as Graham finally thinks to press the reset button and silence the alarm, she says nothing. As he grumbles his expletive-laden resentment into a struggle with his left shoe, she stays quiet. It's only when she hears him shrugging off his coat that she thinks it might be best to speak to him about the missing pantry. She thinks of the words she would use to explain the gaping hole in space that used to be where they kept the cardigans and tinned tomatoes. She follows him to the hallway

'Be careful, babe, the…'

'Me? Be careful? From the woman who I have to stop burning the flat down when she forgets her toast, or fucking curling iron or whatever'

'I don't have a curling iron, Graham, and the straightener was warming up when you unplugged it. You always fucking do this, Graham.' He reaches for the handle. 'You never ask, you just do. And it's never your fault is it? You turn off my straighteners, push me out the door complaining about being late, then bitch all night about how my hair got in your face when we sat next to each other...'

'I don't appreciate the tone, Megs, I really don't.' He's still looking at her, now of all moments he's looking at her. The dark is open now, a foot and a half of dark between the door frame and coat rack. His coat is half off his shoulder. His left hand is on the inside door handle. He has his back to nothingness. And now, he is looking at her.

'Because you refuse to take responsibility for anything I have to just lie down and stay quiet? Is that it?' He just. Keeps. Going. 'Why are you so sensitive? I could deal with the fuck-ups if you just owned them but no, it can't be your fault, can it? You can never just be wrong; you have to sulk and pout like a...'

It was a piercing, fearful and full-throated scream. Yet, it seemed to recede into silence almost as soon as it had come tearing into existence. After a few seconds, all she can hear is the quiet thrumming of empty space.

She notices the chill, not so much a draught but a slowly flowing surge of the air around her being displaced. She looks over the edge of nothing. The coat hook that had strained for so long against its perfunctory attachment by mismatched screws has been torn away. It, along with most of the winter coats are gone.

After a while. She gathers the remaining cardigans and hats, strewn as shrapnel across the hallway floor. She fishes out a scarf trailing into the dark and closes the door to nothingness. She remembers the fridge holds half a roast chicken from last night, she decides reheated chicken would be superior to soup. She tips the carbonite slab under the cooling grill into the bin. Better to burn than fade to nothing she thinks, realising Graham never really deserved 'better'. She knows that Graham would have never believed her anyway. She wonders at which point she will only remember him as dead.

Banu
Naush Sabah

In our quarter the mood was dark,
everyone had tied up their packs.

We would follow our cousins to
find new land, as our people do.

Soon each face became a grave,
we were confined, claustrophobic.

Women wailed and wept while men
whispered prayers in tremulous tones.

Some of our uncles and fathers
were led away by them in groups.

Again, again, they took away more.
None of the previous returned.

The sun slowly sank in the sky,
gurgled cries and metallic scents rose.

My brother was ten months younger,
but his body stronger and wider.

They undid my wrapper and looked
for pubes. I was not man enough.

I clung to my mum and sisters,
watched father and brother look back.

Days later they took us from our city;
a tribe of women, girls, and boys.

At market, split by strength and sex,
next to leathers, clays, camels and goats.

Machine Time
Naush Sabah

Time moves slowly in regular machine-measured beeps,
we watch you lying there, a swollen silent mass,
as colour drains from your plump cheeks.

We've been visiting this room many long weeks,
insouciant at first, while waiting for sickness to pass,
but time moved slow, in regular machine-measured beeps.

Soon you wouldn't eat or move and looked so weak.
While they did biopsies and tests, we'd fret and ask
why colour drains from your plump cheeks.

They sedated and breathed for you. We'd never speak.
We'd wait and we'd hope and were glad as it passed
that time moved in slow, regular, machine-measured beeps.

I crashed on my way there. You, oblivious and asleep.
A horde outside intensive care, sob and amass,
as colour drains from your plump cheeks.

My periods stopped. A year my womb wouldn't weep.
Who can we rage against, or rip at, or ask
why time still moves, slowly, in machine-measured beeps,
since the colour drained from your plump cheeks.

A Stroke Of Misfortune
Portland Jones

They say that life can change in the blink of an eye, the skip of a heartbeat. It took longer than that. Life was ticking along just fine when life itself took a side swipe, knocked me off balance. Nothing I could do but go with the flow and try not to be swept out to sea.

A&E on Friday night is noisy with frustration as clocks tick slower than they have ever tocked before. Alcohol-fuelled tension keeps everyone on edge. My heart was doing its own thing, dancing away to a new tune. It was enjoying its liberation. After two days, it was time to get someone in authority to rein it in. Medication prescribed to sedate this errant heart brought it under control. Success within hours. False sense of security, that's all.

The problem with your heart abdicating its duty is the knock-on effect. Layman's explanation – the irregular beat stirs up debris nestling in the heart's bottom chambers. When heart gets back to work, it merrily pushes this crud around in the blood flow. And that means you are at risk of stroke. This has all been carefully explained to me, aspirin a daily reminder.

Saturday evening placebo TV strobes in the background, laughing happy people interspersed with blasts of adverts. I glance over to my husband of many years to see if now is the right time to cajole him to change channel, turn down the volume, anything to dampen Metallica gigging in my head, headache chasing round and round the cavern that houses my spinning brain. I can't see him properly. It's like looking through a heavily smoked pane of glass, dark grey obscuring his face. Oh fuck.

Visual disturbance. Dizziness. Headache. These are the signs of that stroke they keep warning me about.

'Brian,' I say. 'I think we have a problem.'

OMG I think I'm having a stroke

We've all seen the adverts on TV. FAST. Get help quick before the brain sets on fire. That one. Brian dialled 999 and asked for an ambulance. Paramedics duly attended, bringing a chill breeze from the February air with them along with their oversized bag full of the tricks of their trade.

I explained that I had been in A&E and I was concerned that the symptoms looked like I was having a stroke. They checked my blood pressure, attached sticky pads to my chest took a heart trace.

'History of migraine?' they asked.

'About twenty years ago,' I said.

'It's a migraine headache,' they said. 'Take paracetamol.'

I was stunned.

'Don't you think it might be more serious than that given my history?'

'Calm down,' they said. 'You're getting yourself stressed. That's what's causing the symptoms.'

Hello headache

I took myself to bed to nurse the headache, my new companion who had arrived to stay. Overwhelming tiredness led me to spend more time in bed in a few days than I had in the previous few life-filled months.

I kept going over what had happened. Had I really created these symptoms through anxiety? My sensible, logical brain told me that I hadn't, that I needed help and fast. My tired, damaged brain lost confidence, picked up on the judgment passed on me, didn't know what to do and didn't have the strength to do anything.

I have – correction, had – the greatest of respect for my GP whom I have known for a long time and was wonderful during my mother's decline with dementia. I explained the symptoms, what the paramedics had said about me causing the symptoms by worrying. I'm not a worrier. I take life much as it comes, and I thought my GP knew this, so I wasn't expecting what she said next.

'The paramedics are right, Portland. You need to calm down.'

What I couldn't articulate at the time, which with the clarity of hindsight I now realise very clearly, was that I wasn't worried about having a stroke in the future. I was worried that I'd already had one.

So, I went back home and stayed there for the next four days. In the quiet times, the dark of the night times, I chased thoughts around in my head. What made people see me as a person who created illness from anxiety? I found this disturbing. When did perceptions change so much? I felt vulnerable and at a low ebb.

Someone listened

On Friday – six days after the initial incident – I'd had enough. The headache wasn't going anywhere. Surely even a migraine must go away at some stage.

At five to three in the afternoon, I had an appointment with a doctor whom I had never seen before. She loved my boots – sensible and sturdy, decorated with flowers. She described me as fifty-nine years young. She asked why I was there. I said I needed reassurance; I needed someone to tell me I hadn't had a stroke. She looked at my notes, asked questions.

'Portland, I'm not in a position to give you reassurance. I don't have the information to do that.' She picked up the phone, spoke to the on-call specialist stroke nurse at the local hospital.

'Go straight to A&E and they will see you. If you can get there before five, the stroke doctor will still be there.'

I made it before five. Within an hour, I'd had a CT scan which confirmed I had had a stroke. Six days after that stoke, I had people who were listening to me, giving me the medication I should have had in that critical window just after the stroke.

Was I scared? Of course. When someone says you've had a significant stroke, you don't know how to process that – so many questions. Will I have another one? Will I get better? Some questions you don't want to ask out loud. You don't want to hear the answers.

The hospital staff understand that. They tell you gently, patiently. They brought a computer screen to my bedside, showed me the scan. Pointed out which bit of my brain was affected, dark grey streaks marking the damage at the back, the damage to the vision centre. Tests confirm partial visual field loss.

And there it was gone

So, what does damage to that part of your brain look like?

I seem to have a black hole in the top left of my vision where things disappear to. More puzzling than not seeing things is seeing things that aren't there – visual hallucinations. The doctor described it as Phantom Limb Syndrome for my vision. The brain knows there is missing information, so it fills the gap with information drawn from elsewhere, often totally unrelated scenarios. I find myself ducking from objects flying across the room or trying to bat them away. My mantra for several days was: 'They are not ghosts. They are not ghosts.' There's nothing there.

The rest was yet to come, yet to filter through the general unsettledness.

Home again, home again, jiggity jig.

Going home from hospital is being turned out on your own in the wilderness. The physio did tests. I can walk upstairs, turn around and walk back down with no problems. I can touch my nose with my finger, even with my eyes shut. I can stand on one leg with only a hint of a wobble. I can remember what day it is and where I am. I can join dots.

The other problems aren't so obvious and can't be evaluated, measured, ticked off someone's list. I didn't even notice at first. When you clean a room, you start with the empty boxes you are tripping over before you pick up the Lego bricks buried in the carpet, but at the end of the day, when you settle down to rest in your PJs, it's the persistent unsuspected assaults on your feet that make life difficult.

Leaving hospital was the next stage in my journey from the old me to the new me, whoever she may be.

Driving is freedom, independence, a social life. Being dependent on others is taking a lot of adjusting. There's much commitment from others, freely given. No need to ask. I am touched and so blessed.

The list of things I struggle with seems endless – reading, understanding numbers, remembering anything – including the long words that describe my problems. Prosopagnosia is the ability to recognise faces which I can no longer do. Quadrantanopia is the precise description of my visual field loss. I get lost. Frequently. Loss of concentration affects everything – cooking is now a H&S risk. I have burned more things in the two years since my stroke than I ever did in all the years previous. Neuro-fatigue shortens every day. Thinking makes me tired, reading makes me tired, feeling sorry for myself is exhausting.

Life is such joy at the moment.

Actually, it really is.

What happens next?
You wait and wonder.

You wait to see if there is any improvement, any deterioration. You wait to see if one day soon you will go a whole day without a headache, without feeling exhausted and needing a nap. You wait to see if you will feel anything like your pre-stroke self anytime soon. You wait for the review with your consultant – 1st June. You wait for the assessment of your vision, so you have some idea of your potential future. You wait to see if you will have another stroke.

You wander the hinterland, trying to find your way back to certainty, to the person you once were. There is no map to take you there, no sat nav that guides you to the person you used to be. Glimpses keep you searching but the pictures fade to sepia; were you ever the person you think you might have been? The images change from who you were, to focus instead on who you are not. I no longer see myself drumming with the band; I see the djembe forlorn in the corner. I see myself unemployed, unemployable, twenty-five years of fighting homelessness discarded. Facebook brings me daily memories of the old me. I am amazed. Did I really do that? I cry. Often, easily. (Did I mention that emotional lability is a side effect of stroke?) I confess I am particularly fond of the photo of that woman crashed out face down in the ashes of the campsite fire on the day we danced morris at Stonehenge. That was me?

Rehab in the leafy surrounds of bohemian Moseley forced me out of hiding, forced me to explore this strange unknowable no-man's land. My mission was to find the truth among the teachings that would let me see my future.

The truth, as all truths, was hard. There is no recovery, only coping. There is no return to who you were. There is but one way forward – embrace the new you.

Balkan Chess

Max Mulgrew

In deceptive shade
where battered chessmen
want decisions to be made,
diagonals triangulate

old slivovitz supplies,
sweaty tobacco smoke,
olive trees, dusty vines
and grimy Kalashnikovs.

Pale scorpions pray
under tombstone rocks
where too many players
of reckless games

peep out on times
when elephants trod,
with hopeless smiles,
on Tito's delicate toes.

Bone fragments meld
with limestone karst
- calcified husks blown
from Jurassic wars

when raging storms
tore mountains apart
and tattered uniforms
bled on dry-stone walls.

Cigarette mouths cough
over chequered boards
while the low sun scoffs
over sacrificed pawns.

Something Normal

Charlotte McCormac

Like an unwanted gift,
daylight caught him up
and thrust devotion upon him.
Under the bed,
it hid, torn open.

The gift couldn't be refused. He accepted
affection. Then tried to exchange it.
Tried a new costume instead.
Something normal.
Waited until he felt ready
to wear his rainbow stripes.

Sink or Swim
Melanie Dillon

As I wedge the thermometer back between the ridges of the radiator, I wonder whether adding talcum powder to my already artfully-paled face would have the desired effect or simply be overkill. Deciding that it'll probably be worth the risk – any flakes could only add to the general aura of sickness after all – I'm about to get out of bed for a rummage in the bathroom cabinet when I hear Mum's footsteps on the stairs again. Hastily rearranging the blankets and tucking the still only lukewarm thermometer (damned inefficient central heating) in the corner of my mouth, I put on my best woe-is-me look just as the bedroom door opens and Mum strides in.

'Sorry, love. I've just had a call from Sandra in the office and they're snowed under with work, so I really do have to go in. Can't be helped, I'm afraid.'

Her sympathetic words are slightly negated by the fact that she's already pulling the various components of my school uniform out of my drawers and wardrobe. She hasn't even checked my (only slightly-faked) temperature!

'But Mum,' I whine, 'I'm sick.' Or at least I'm trying to be.

'Don't whine, Claire.'

Damn it.

'You can't be that sick – you ate half that pizza last night.' Uniform safely gathered, she drapes the lot over the back of my chair and starts digging around in the bottom of my wardrobe. 'It's swimming today isn't it, love? That'll make you feel better. Good bit of exercise. Here we go.' She finally unearths my PE kit from a pile of jeans and at long last turns to regard her poor invalid daughter. I try to look pathetic.

'I'm sorry, Claire. Really I am.'

Guilt. Success!

'If it was any other day I'd stay home with you, but they really need me at work and since your Dad…well, you know we haven't exactly had money to spare.'

Guilt reversed. I'm screwed.

'Tell you what. If you still feel bad at dinner time give me a ring and I'll come pick you up, okay?'

Not okay. Swimming's first thing. By dinner time it'll be too late. But Mum's got that anxious look in her eyes that's become so familiar since Dad left. Since he decided that instead of a steady job and a family who loved him, what he *really* needed to make his life complete was a commune in Dorset and a massage therapist named Stardust.

I know I've lost the argument though and I feel too sorry for Mum to make a big fuss. So, with only a few put-on sighs (I am entitled), I reluctantly drag myself out of my fake sick bed and prepare for another day at school. And another swimming lesson.

Who knows, I try to tell myself in a positive-thinking kinda way as Mum goes downstairs to get breakfast. Maybe today won't be all that bad. Maybe they'll leave me alone for once, go torment some other kid for a change. Maybe the pool will be closed for drainage after some kid went to the loo in it during the mother and toddler splash-a-thon. Maybe aliens will attack at some point between now and 9.15. Anything could happen. Just please God don't make me have my swimming lesson.

***

Okay, now I know for sure – there is no God. What kind of almighty benevolent being wouldn't answer a desperate teenage girl's plea and cancel her swimming lesson? It's not like I asked for world peace or anything major like that. So that's it. Final proof. If God couldn't do that one teeny tiny thing for me then he doesn't exist. End of.

Splat. A spit ball of rolled up tissue hits the back of my neck, no doubt forming a nice little pattern alongside the marks from the paperclips and rubber bands that have already hit their intended targets so expertly in the five minutes since the coach left school.

As always, I refuse to give my tormentors the satisfaction of seeing my face and keep staring resolutely at the ghastly-patterned seat-back in front of me. The giggles and taunts are barely audible over the general ruckus that accompanies our every trip to the pool, but then I hear another unmistakable splat, though I feel no corresponding ickiness on my neck.

'WHO DID THAT?' bellows Mr Jackson, rising like a sea monster from the depths of the seat in front of me. The entire coach is instantly silent. I shrink down in my seat as Mr Jackson storms past me down the aisle to where Becky and her gang are hastily trying to hide their pilfered McDonald's straws up the sleeves of their jumpers.

'Becky Grimble! Are you responsible for this disgusting behaviour?'

'No, Sir. It wasn't me. Honest. It must've been the boys, Sir.'

'Nuh-uh. Lying cow. Saw her do it, Sir. She were aiming at that geeky kid but hit you instead.'

That can only be Ralph Jones, star of the football team and on-off boyfriend to Becky Grimble herself. Today must be an off day.

'Punk!' Becky roars. 'Asshole! See if you get any next time you come sniffing round. I ain't putting out for no loser!'

'That's not what I heard!' yells another voice further up the coach, followed swiftly by Mr Jackson yelling, 'Sit down Becky! And you Jamel. All of you just stay in your seats. Look, we're here now. Becky, I want you in my class this morning, so I can keep an eye on you. Any more trouble and I'll be calling your parents.'

The coach erupts with jeers but all I can think is that my one safety net is gone. Becky, the same Becky who hates my guts and who makes it her mission in life to make *my* life hell, is going to be in the same swimming class as me. That's it. I'm dead.

***

We've had swimming lessons once a week for over a year now and so far, no-one has noticed that I've been faking my lack of swimming ability. The reason is simple: Becky is a good swimmer and therefore in the upper class. By pretending to flounder, I can stay at the opposite end of the pool, hidden from Becky's torments amid the general chaos and near drownings of the Beginners' group. Until today.

Keeping my eyes fixed firmly on my feet, I scurry off the coach and into the girls' changing rooms to bag myself a cubicle. Thankfully, the walls go floor to ceiling. If they didn't, I've no doubt that Becky and co would peek under or over, furthering my misery. Still, as always, I've put my swimming costume on underneath my uniform so I'm changed and into the pool before there's any chance of trouble.

Normally, if I've made it this far I know I'll be okay. The Beginners' class finishes before the Advanced one, so I can usually get changed before most of the other girls get out of the water. On any other day I'd be the only girl in the Beginners' swimming group, which suits me fine. The boys don't bother me much, just the occasional insult. They leave the worst to Becky and her mates.

There used to be another girl in the group with me. Maybelle. She was new to our school and only lasted a week. The one and only time she came swimming with us she took one look at the water and started screaming. No-one could get her to stop. The whole class stared, treading water while she screamed. Mr Jackson had to call some doctor who injected her, and then she fainted. She didn't come to school after that.

By the look of it, no such distraction is going to present itself today. Some of the boys are already in the shallow end, but thankfully there's no sign of Becky. I grab a float from the multi-coloured pile by the door (got to keep up the act) and ease down into the water. Mr Jackson is already doing his customary bellow at a group of boys who are attempting to flood the tiles over by the steps. I start doing my usual half waddle, half swim across the pool, knowing that if I can keep up the pretence and stay quiet then Mr Jackson and the boys will leave me alone, all assuming that I'm just a very slow learner.

But then I see Becky emerge from the changing rooms and slowly make her way towards the shallow end of the pool, her gaze fixed on me. I try to concentrate on faking my poor swimming ability and only dimly hear Mr Jackson tell Becky to do laps and stay out of trouble. But I know he's far too busy trying to stop the boys from either drowning each other or flooding the place to really pay any attention to her.

Becky starts swimming laps. Just like me. She's swimming properly of course, not a float in sight, and I remind myself to keep up the illusion of aquatic incompetence. Throwing away the float and showing my newly-discovered swimming ability might get me moved up to the Advanced group and out of harm's way today, but it would be bound to make things worse when Becky goes back to her regular group next week. So, I keep the float and the lie, weaving between the boys' water fight and managing to avoid Becky on my first two waddle-swim lengths. But on the third, she corners me at the opposite end of the pool, far away from Mr Jackson and any form of help. She doesn't say anything, just calmly reaches out and knocks my float aside. I keep quiet. The water's shallow enough to stand up in anyway, and surely she can't do anything that bad in a crowded pool. Right?

Then I see the glint in her eyes, of a predator finally catching its prey, and I'm terrified. Becky lunges out, grabs both my shoulders and plunges me under the water. Instinct surges through me and I try to kick her away, to scream for help, but her legs twist around mine and I only end up swallowing a load of water. She's ducked down in the water now as well and is regarding me calmly, her body pinning me still as I struggle to breathe, to escape. As she's almost twice my size this is a fight I have little chance of winning.

Then, without warning, she leans in and kisses me – full on the mouth. A puff of desperately needed air. One second. Two. Three. Hot pressure on my lips, life in my lungs. And then she let's go. We both pop back up in the water. Before I can even get my breath back – or is it her breath now? – Becky's already swimming another lap, Mr Jackson and the boys oblivious to what just happened.

For a moment I just stand there. I think of all the years of torment that Becky and her friends have put me through. The name-calling, hair-pulling, tripping-up, spit-ball throwing hell of it all. And then I think of her kiss, her mouth on mine.

And leaving the float where she threw it, I kick off from the edge and swim, properly swim, across the pool after Becky.

Borderlands
Kristof B. Marton

FADE IN:

EXT. LANDSCAPE VIEW, AUSTRO-HUNGARIAN BORDERLANDS
- DUSK

Winter, 2018. A train RUSHES along the rail track.

A vast, peaceful and snowy field on its southern
side and a forest to the north.

INT. TRAIN DRIVER'S CABIN - DUSK

'Happy Retirement' and '40 Years of Service'
labels decorate the wall.

A huge BOTTLE OF CHAMPAGNE in a Tesco bag.

OLD PHOTO of a smiling young man hangs from above.
He's holding a certificate next to a red train.

LASZLO (male, 63) sits in a chair at the control
panel.

Bald on top. Semi-long hair at the sides. Stubbly
beard. Old-school glasses and blue train driver's
uniform.

Straight face. He stares at the landscape ahead.

Light snowfall.

His eyes wander to the old photo.

He sighs.

A KNOCK on the door behind him.

                    LASZLO
          Ye?

ENDRE (male, 57) enters. Blue suit and tie. He
holds a small ticket printer machine in his right
hand.

                    ENDRE
          I found one hiding in the toilet…
          Can't believe they think that
          still works.

Endre looks around the cabin.

                    ENDRE (CONT'D)
          Bet ya could drive this blindfold,
          huh?

Laszlo turns.

                    LASZLO
          Kinda.

Endre giggles.

Laszlo sets his eyes back on the track.

Endre exits the cabin.

Laszlo knit his brows.

                    LASZLO (CONT'D)
          FUCK!

50 meters ahead, SOMEONE IN A GREEN COAT stands on
the track.

Laszlo PULLS the emergency break.

Squeeeeeeeeeeeaaaaak!

The train SLOWS DOWN with an awful squeal.

A horn BLARES.

The bottle of champagne FALLS, ROLLS away and HITS
the wall.

It BREAKS.

BUMP!

The train hits something.

The train still ROLLS…

It stops.

Laszlo looks out of the window.

He tries to say something.

Inaudible.

EXT. NEAR THE TRAIN - NIGHT

The vehicle stands still on the rails.

PASSENGERS on their phones.

Some of them light fags or already smoke anxiously.

A few wander aimlessly.

Two POLICEMEN walk around and question them.

EXT. RAILWAY AT BORDERLANDS - NIGHT

Police, Ambulance and Railway crew SEARCH along the rails. Flashlights ON.

LASZLO and ENDRE follow them.

A fresh bandage wrapped around Endre's head.

Laszlo PLODS with a blank face.

He stares at the ground.

A few more steps…

Laszlo COLLAPSES on the ground.

He SOBS.

The search team don't notice.

They go further.

Endre CROUCHES and PUTS his arm around Laszlo's shoulder.

A long moment of silence.

Laszlo regains his balance.

Endre LIFTS him up.

They look around.

The search team is far away.

They turn back towards the train.

A few STEPS…

Endre SPOTS GREEN FABRIC in the snow on the other side of the Rail.

He points towards it.

>   ENDRE
>   Laci!

Laszlo's eyes follow.

They CREEP over the rails.

They stop in front of a big PILE OF SNOW.

Laszlo GRABS the GREEN FABRIC and PULLS it…

It's a GREEN JACKET.

>   LASZLO
>   What the...?

They look around thoroughly.

Only a few meters away…

A CARROT, plunged straight into the snow.

INT. TRAIN DRIVER'S CABIN - NIGHT

The engines are silent.

Laszlo SPRINGS UP from his chair.

Then SMASHES on his command desk.

He TEARS OFF the 'Happy Retirement' and '40 Years of Service' Decorations.

He GASPS.

Deep breath.

COUGHS.

He bends down to reach the mic.

PRESSES the button.

> LASZLO
> Ladies and gentlemen, as you
> surely know, we hit a…

Laszlo RELEASES the button.

He utters a queer, high-pitched CHUCKLE.

Then PRESSES the button again.

> LASZLO (CONT'D)
> There was an accident. The train
> will now continue to the next
> Station.

Laszlo SWALLOWS.

> LASZLO (CONT'D)
> Thank you for choosing Hungarian
> State Railways.

FADE OUT.

Tunnel

A Fibonacci Sequence

Rebecca Wright

Walk
through,
past the
canal, and
into the depths of
the tunnel. Spiders shrivel in
the watery, cracking ceiling. Bow your head. Grip your
hands on the rusted metal that protects your flesh from the
    clotted and thirsty canal.
Your eyes adjust to the darkness surrounding your frame.
    Eyelashes clump with dust. Rapid insects scuttle. Fur catches
    your leg. Hair on your arms
flush against the cotton of your fraying jacket. Heavy,
    stumbling feet. Sweaty face.
Hold your breath. Trapped between two bodies of harsh nature.
Keep walking. Fragments of wall follow
on your clothing. Brittle
stone against
raw skin.
Then
you're
out.

The Union Flag in Semaphore

Adrian B. Earle

Isosceles angles of deepest blue/ as
distant on the spectrum both
visibly & politically
from bands of vibrant red/ drawing
as always to the centre
separated/ or perhaps unified
by an all-pervasive/ angular structure
of/
Whiteness
bold enough to scar continents
fragile enough to ripple in the wind
they /say the people/ make the country
they say the people make it
& the flag defines it.

Knock Once For Yes

Olivia Hodgson

Knock once for yes;
my love: I can't hear you
when muffled between
bathroom tile and porcelain
made bare by nights scarred
in acid-washed palms.

Syllable-soft is enough: let it
smooth over two hemispheres,
like a newborn's head-in-waiting;
to halo your halves into one.

Rest your already wisped spirit
later, after woodchip and black coffee
suppress our damp a little more.
And yet,

dawn slices the skin on my amniotic
calm – day bursts in, conjuring
hell in a mind-mottled room.

I knit and weave hushes to bind
what's already split; lick begs
into long-healed scars.
No replies. Sunken and raving
once more, so I catch my armour

and lie awake between
two unsettled men.

The Mourning Key
Olivia Hodgson

Mother died yesterday: of that, Mara was absolutely sure.

There was no hesitancy in that passing. The plans had been made for months and Mother had nailed her own Mourning Key to her old headboard. It was something she'd read about years ago and this past week insisted upon. Her cannula would catch during that painful business of winding the twigs until, finally, she announced to an empty room that she was finished. Hammering in the already bent iron nail with the heel of a shoe, the mourning key hung like a Renaissance halo above this jaundiced saint's head.

Mourning Keys are not shaped as you would imagine, or how Mara had expected. The dying must make their own by forcing something that should probably have stayed on the bonfire into a circular, twisted shape. The flowers of the season must decorate its perimeter. Mother's key was dressed only with sewing needles piercing the twigs; each a slice of nickel dangling with navy thread. At the end of each thread were no flowers, but berries: each as pungent and bursting as drops of blood.

What the Mourning Key opens exactly, when it's nailed immobile at the top of the headboard, is the one thing she didn't have a chance to explain.

Mara turned the thing over in her hands as if she were trying not to upset it. It was not much bigger than the span of her hand; not quite wide enough to be a crown. Somehow, it carried a weightlessness that actually added to its presence. The sharp slam of the door-knocker and the family on the other side of it trained her into reverence. After habitually tying her hair back and pulling down the hem of her dress, she returned the creation to the bent iron nail and descended the stairs of her Mother's Father's house. She would now call him this, rather than 'Grandad', since the discovery of her adoption papers in the paper-weighted hush of the attic.

Downstairs looked like a murder scene without the body. Furniture was upturned or crouching above her, always above her, on tabletops and boxes, protected from a flood that would never come. The house cradled the dry silence of a church. Diligently, Mara had passed from room to room covering their rigid forms with blank dust sheets, perhaps to protect the odd air from nurturing them into idols and gargoyles.

Georgia, her cousin, appeared in the hallway before Mara even had a chance to reach the door handle. She didn't even know there was another key cut.

The expectant faces of family members waiting to be catered for were standing behind her. They patted Mara's shoulder or smoothed her hair, before mumbling their way into the kitchen for the important business of removing their food from its cling film.

'I didn't know that you wanted to come,' she said to Georgia.

'I changed my mind.'

Rarely present when married, but always the infant once more when divorced, Georgia seemed to have a particular bent for putting an ocean between herself and what was left of her family. Despite owing much to Mara's Mother, she'd disappear to airport lounges and the hospitality of an in-law. However, she'd soon dry up whatever seabed she had created once rendered husbandless.

She 'kissed' Mara simply by touching cheeks and making a noise with her pursed lips. Someone in the kitchen raised a wine glass as big as a fist in offering. Georgia declined, shaking her head slowly and dabbing the corner of her eyes with a scented tissue.

'Where is *your* husband?' Mara heard, as Georgia followed her up the stairs.

'Out,' she replied.

Mara tidied her Mother's hair and put the make-up in place with the help of her cousin. Georgia had given up affecting tears once they were privately dressing and wrapping the beaded Flamenco scarves around unhelpful limbs.

Mother had spent the first twelve years of her life in Cádiz in the Andalusian region of Spain. No semblance of her early life there had been crafted into Mara's childhood. Colours and rituals were always dimmed. The only filter through which the children were allowed to see her amputated past life was through the morning sunlight touching the clay pots of hibiscus and Spanish basil. Why should she lose that tangibility, that knot around her earliest years under arid sun, for this fable of the Mourning Key that barely belonged anywhere? It was a mystery that dripped longingly like candle wax. Mara's questions had hit the walls of another empty room. She had foraged through the boxes. She couldn't find anything that once belonged to her or her cousin.

'How did it happen?' Georgia asked.

Mara repeated the succinct explanation: she simply slept, then never woke up. Most things weren't out of place yesterday morning, as if death had kindly left them alone. The sheets were undisturbed, and the bedroom door still closed. The only thing she could not account for, the only oddity that had tightened her grip on the door handle, was the blaring light that greeted her through the window. The curtains had been pulled hard off their rungs, pooling in a neat circle on the floor.

And then, the thorns – pushed all the way through the cotton curtains like exit wounds.

After hosting the mourners camped in the kitchen, among bitten nails and sobs half-forced, Mara settled in the lone wing-back chair for Georgia's attempts at memory recall. She asked if Mara could remember the dear little sweet shop; the huge bath towels they had both been warmed with; the spicy Iberian paste that had made her sneeze. Mara's mind, however, was repeatedly answering the earlier question.

She knew where her husband was. He had disappeared behind the pub door, arm in arm, no need for persuasion: the sky hard against her cinder-red hair, parted slightly from the crown and bunched up, like it needed to be out of the way ready for some emergency. There had been no single peak, no point to pick from. No confrontation. Success in marriage is an ongoing practice, as where 'failed' is a single event.

Mara pulled a mattress into Mother's bedroom later that night. Thankfully, everyone had returned to their hotels with little encouragement and did not want to keep vigil. Have you ever slept in the same room as someone who never woke up? They're still there in the morning – same position, bedsheets still cool. One of Mother's hands was still peaking from underneath her duvet, as if feeling for rain.

On her way to the bathroom, Mara found the only satin Flamenco scarf left to wrap around her. Bright and smooth, like freshly polished gold – once the colour of Mother's suntan. The hearse with its wicker coffin would be there in an hour. She was pulling the veil over reality a little lower; crawling back from the cold of this wet, grey island. She let the tap fill the glass to the brim with water.

Mara opened the bedroom door. The glass fell without smashing. Mother was not in bed.

Knelt up, leaning over the white sheets: her strained face in permanent rigor mortis, as if always about to speak. Hands clasped – praying towards the Mourning Key.

Wake

Max Mulgrew

each bird kept secrets
   no whispers
as the tide brought bodies
   rolling
into the tangle
   corpses carried gently
from storms
to curtains
   of cloud
in a moon's phase
   life is done
   ~~~
we stand against
the dying
night
caught before the sun
   between
   the blinding dark
   and blinding light
deciding on lines
   that wash
   the shingle and
chill our feet

High and Dry
Ravenna Alcott

'I erd' he killed a man.'

'Old-Boat-Brown?'

'With his hands, I heard - like an animal!'

'Tossed the body into the sea!'

'No! Pol-from-the-Chippy said rape. Drowned her in the end.'

'Our Michael said the same. Weren't just one woman neither.'

'Well, I bumped into Big Dave at The Ol' Bottle and he reckon' it was a kiddie thing.'

'It's true! My brother's nephew's friend knew the girl!'

'How dreadful!'

'He's a monster!'

***

The old man's constant state of solitude bothered people. His peculiarities made them uneasy and his appearance only succeeded in aggravating what they already disliked.

Despite the decades that had passed, he wore the same clothes. A shirt that hung heavy against the protruding rungs of his ribs, the cloth now discoloured from sweat and harsh weather. His trousers were tied at the waist by a piece of cable that dragged behind him in the sand; sometimes he would trip but he never thought to cut it. His hair was wild, like a washed-up pile of frayed fishing rope. Often, on gusty days, his hair would get trapped between his remaining teeth, scaring the children. His teeth were yellow and sharp, like his toenails, that had punctured through the brittle leather of his boots which were held together by tape and string. Old-Boat-Brown was jaded and bent to the point of breaking but his boat, his boat was in perfect condition.

The gloss of the hull shone in the soft sun of June, without a single scratch interrupting the glass-like finish. Above, the mast stood strong on the deck, the silver bolts holding it in place had been polished and the rigging pulled tight in neat knots and bows. The deck itself had been swabbed and varnished, its timber lying tight and compact without a single splinter breaking the ranks.

He would check the boat obsessively. Often, he'd be found crawling on all fours with his face pressed into the sand, brushing and polishing the keel until he reached the skeg at the back. After a while, Brown would have circled the boat so many times, for so many hours, that he'd form a trench.

Fishermen would lay bets on the boat toppling, 'Double or nothin' that the mast snaps like a cocktail stick!' they'd say.

At sunset, a throng of merry men would stumble out of *The Old Bottle* and stagger across the sands, only to return empty handed once again, cursing at the marigold sky.

Sometimes, Brown would stop and mutter things too, eyes bulging with his hands hovering over the hull. He'd have conversations with it, with his ear pressed firmly against the bow of the boat. His wrinkled forehead would sit like a stack of paper, as if he was concentrating. Occasionally, his eyes would pop open like a camera shutter, making the tourists drop their ice creams as they passed.

He'd say, 'Their bones lie greening on the seafloor. But their souls got stuck in the boat!'

When the distressed travellers carried on walking, he'd smile. 'I don't mind being mad, it means I loved the hardest.'

One day, Old-Boat-Brown's body was found.

Witnesses said he had been circling the boat more frantically than usual. This time, the trench that formed was too deep, the sand shifted and the boat crushed him.

The fishermen's pockets weren't so empty that day.

A pack of locals went to the funeral, as none of them had ever been to a killer's funeral before. It was a short service, led by a flustered vicar who saw Brown's corpse as a very rude interruption to his day's plans, from his agitated squints at the clock tower and his rushed mumble of the Lord's prayer.

The locals left quickly, soon realising that a murderer's funeral was just like any other.

The vicar belched and said, 'A devoted husband to wife Amelia, and loving Father to Molly who both drowned tragically on a family fishing trip on Old Boat Brown. Now may you rest, Arthur John Browning.'

After skipping several verses of the psalms, the vicar looked up to find himself alone in the churchyard. Hurriedly, he performed the sign of the cross and disappeared down the church path.

The Cut

Ravenna Alcott

She's like spilt
ink. Running
beneath our
smoke. Mother
of Metal who
carried our
bulk.

Close friends with the Bridge and
his pigeons who coo her to sleep.

She keeps your
secrets wedged
within
her algae-covered
bricks.
Her jewels of
broken glass
glisten at her
towpaths.
She doesn't
like makeup.
Still, boys
stain her face
with colours
that do not
suit her.

A lad slipped
and now sleeps
in her
blackened
bodice.
But her waters
are patient.
Enduring:
your tears,
your piss,
your shit.
Her levels
rise when she
feels a dead
rat on her
embankment.
Her locks
gush.
Lovers
shhhhhhhh
hhhhhhh
hhhh
hhh
hh
h
h
h
.

.

.

Fitting In
Abbie Thay

FADE IN:

EXT. BIRMINGHAM - DAY

A black Range Rover pulls over. Two teenage girls
jump out of the car.

LIBBY GREEN (14, smartly dressed, innocent-
looking) pops her head in the car window.

JOHN GREEN (46) hands her some money.

> JOHN
> Here, treat yourself to some new
> shoes? Maybe a jacket?
> (beat)
> Bras?

> LIBBY
> Thanks, Dad. But please don't ever
> say bras again.

> JOHN
> Dad error. Do you remember the
> rules?

> LIBBY
> Don't speak to creepy men, text
> you once every hour, and don't do
> anything I don't want to.
>
> (beat)
>
> So can you pick us up at
> four-thirty?

                    JOHN
          Sure, kiddo. You know that girl
          you're with, is she from school?

                    LIBBY
          Four-thirty, Dad.

Libby walks away. John BEEPS and waves as he
drives off.

MACKENZIE ROWLEY (17, chav, short skirt) links her
arm through Libby's as they walk together.

INT. BIRMINGHAM BULLRING - DAY

Midday crowds. Libby is holding several shopping
bags.

Mackenzie is holding one Primark bag. They sip on
McDonald's milkshakes as they walk into -

INT. NEW LOOK - DAY

Mackenzie smiles at the SECURITY GUARD (young, fat
and sweaty). He pays them no attention, engrossed
in his phone.

ON HIS PHONE: FIFA

Mackenzie holds up a dress against her body in the
mirror.

                    MACKENZIE
          Oh MY god! This dress is gorgeous.

          And like, so me!

                    LIBBY
          That is so glittery!

                    MACKENZIE
          Try the pink one!

                    LIBBY
          My parents would never let me wear
          something like that.

Mackenzie rolls her eyes and puts the dress up against Libby's body.

> MACKENZIE
> But don't you think you look so
> pretty?

Libby tilts her head.

IN THE MIRROR: She looks at her reflection.

> LIBBY
> (smiling)
> I do feel pretty!

Mackenzie gestures a 10/10 with her hands.

> MACKENZIE
> I bet Kyle would notice you in a
> dress like that. He's a bit older,
> ain't he? He likes mature girls.

Mackenzie twirls Libby around.

They check the price tag. Their eyes go wide.

Libby turns her purse upside down. Nothing.
Mackenzie SIGHS.

> LIBBY
> Maybe we can come back in a few
> weeks?

> MACKENZIE
> Easy for you. Mum is drinking
> again so my wages will be spent on
> booze, booze and oh, more booze.

Libby fiddles with her hands. The girls slouch back on the mannequin stool. They sip their milkshakes that are almost empty. There is just a CRACKING noise.

Mackenzie looks over at the security guard.

He is chatting up two younger women.

>   MACKENZIE
>   You know? If you want to impress
>   Kyle so much, you could slip the
>   dresses in your bag.

Libby SPITS out her milkshake. Several shoppers
look at her in disgust and move away.

>   LIBBY
>   What! No way! I would get into so
>   much trouble.

>   MACKENZIE
>   There it is, the Daddy's girl.

>   LIBBY
>   I'm not. I just couldn't steal.

>   MACKENZIE
>   Everyone can steal, Lib.
>   (beat)
>   Watch this.

Mackenzie grabs a pair of earrings and rips the
tag off.

She looks around.

She drops them into one of Libby's bags.

>   LIBBY
>   Mackenzie!

>   MACKENZIE
>   Sh! See, you just stole!

Libby dives her hand into the bag. Mackenzie GRABS
her wrist to stop her.

>   MACKENZIE
>   Did anybody see?

>   LIBBY
>   Well, no. But -

> MACKENZIE
> Nobody saw! And you have a new
> pair of earrings. Bonus.

Libby looks over at the security guard. He has
his eyes closed, headphones in and humming to his
music.

> MACKENZIE
> Walk out the store now and see for
> yourself. No alarms will go off,
> I promise. Do it. Go!

Mackenzie pushes Libby forward. Libby takes a deep
breath.

She walks out the shop with her eyes closed.

No alarms.

She runs back to Mackenzie. They burst out
laughing.

> LIBBY
> (covering her mouth)
> I can't believe I just did that!

> MACKENZIE
> You should really show your fun
> side more. It suits you.
> (beat)
> Now the dresses.

Libby rubs her fingers on the dress. She shakes her
head.

> LIBBY
> A dress is way different to a pair
> of earrings. I'm sorry.

> MACKENZIE
> It would be such a cool story to
> tell everyone. Especially that
> older lad you fancy.
> (beat)

I heard he steals to.

Libby SIGHS and gazes at the dresses.

She GRABS them and rips the price tags off.

Shoves them in her bag. Heads towards the exit.

Mackenzie runs after her and links her arm.

The SECURITY TAG is slightly hanging out the side of her bag.

The girls nod at the security guard, giggling. He takes his headphones out and watches them leave. His eyes squinting.

They walk through the scanners –

BEEP BEEP BEEP

Red lights flash. Everyone turns to stare.

> SECURITY GUARD #1
> Oi! You two. Wait there!

> MACKENZIE
> Run! Now!

Libby and Mackenzie sprint out of the store.

INT - BIRMINGHAM BULLRING - DAY

The security guard chases after them.

> SECURITY GUARD #1
> (into his radio)
> We got a code 416. Ground floor!

Libby and Mackenzie barge past shoppers, knocking them over.

People jump out of the way.

The security guard keeps stopping to catch his breath.

The girls slam the exit doors open, smiling.

EXT. BIRMINGHAM BULLRING - MOMENTS LATER

Another SECURITY GUARD jumps in front of the girls.

                    SECURITY GUARD #2
           STOP! Open your bags, girls. Now!

John's Range Rover pulls up at the side of the road.

He JUMPS out of the car and races towards them. Libby looks at her watch. 4.30pm.

                    JOHN
           Excuse me! That's MY daughter!

Security guard #1 flies out the doors. He places his hands on his knees. He struggles to even talk.

                    SECURITY GUARD #2
           Looks like your daughter has been
           stealing, Sir!

                    JOHN
           Not my kid. Show him Lib, and your
           friend.

Libby opens her bag. Inside are the stolen items. She sobs.

John steps back and covers his mouth in shock.

Mackenzie opens her bag. Nothing. She smiles at John.

Security guard #2 snatches the stolen items back. He then assists the other guard in catching his breath.

                    SECURITY GUARD #2
           I'll leave this one with you, Sir.

           This guy is gonna pass out.

The guards hobble away. John grabs Libby by her blouse and chucks her in the car. Mackenzie trails behind, smirking.

John slams the door and leans up against the car, burying his head in his hands.

He speeds off in the distance.

FADE OUT.

Blood Upon the Rose

Danny Maguire

'Joseph, you're gonna get yourself killed!'

That was the last thing his sister said to him before he closed the front door and went to join the march. His mom had told him he wasn't allowed to go, but she was at Aunt Marie's house and didn't need to know. He told Ava that if she rang Mom and told on him, he'd tell the soldiers that she was working with the Ra.

He wore his green and white Christmas jumper despite the season being over a month ago, but it was the only green jumper he had. He couldn't wear a t-shirt because it was still way too cold. He didn't wear a coat or a jacket; he had a feeling the crowd would be big enough to keep him warm.

He found the march as it made its way down the Lecky Road, just off Dove Gardens. The road was filled with people, from the row of house to the grassy hills along the other side. At the junction of Westland Street, Joseph could see a lorry leading the march. He'd heard it was to be used for speeches when they got to Free Derry Corner.

He looked around for his friends. There was a small gap between the crowd and front doors, so Joseph decided to run; up the road, alongside the marchers singing *The Men Behind the Wire*, looking for his friends.

He spied bright orange hair as someone was pushed out of the crowd. It was Kevin. Never had he seen someone look more like a leprechaun, with his flaming hair and a patriotic emerald green suit. All he was missing was a top hat and a shillelagh. If it wasn't for the green, he'd look like a beacon for the Orange Order. Kevin picked himself up and, with a grin on his face, dived back into the crowd.

Joseph followed him and found Kevin and Sean having a wrestling match whilst marching. Joseph gave Sean's arse a kick and the boys jumped in surprise. Instead of being greeted, Joseph immediately found himself in a headlock, head stuck under Kevin's armpit.

The march was the most fun he had had in a long time. Just walking along the road itself felt freeing. He had only heard about the protests from other people. They told him about how marching for their freedom from the English proddies, for their country, was both important and enjoyable. Joseph had never done anything for a cause in his life until now, and he saw that what he was told was right. Being surrounded by so many people, all of them marching for the same cause, all of them smiling, joking and singing. It gave him a sense of camaraderie, of friendship. Some he knew as friends, neighbours, shopkeepers and butchers, but others he didn't know; but they felt like family too. Being next to Kevin and Sean, his brothers in all but blood, gave him the warmest feeling. Not only was he marching for the cause with his brothers, but he was loving every second of it.

They turned left onto Westland Street, marched all the way past Bulcher Street, up to the roundabout and along Lone Moor Road. At each corner, they were joined by more people. Every direction Joseph looked there was just a sea of people. Some were singing and joking, others talking about what had happened. Kevin's cousin Robert and his uncle Thomas had been taken on the first night. The Soldiers broke into their house, dragged them both out of their beds and took them away.

'It's been five months with no charge or trial. Aunt Frances doesn't know what to do with herself,' Kevin said. 'She can barely get by anymore, what with Uncle Tommy being the one who worked. She's got little Aoife to look after, so she can't go get work, can she?'

'They're bastards,' said Sean. 'The lot of them. English scum.'

'How's she surviving then?' Joseph asked.

'The family's supporting her, aren't they?' said Kevin. 'They have to. No one's gonna let her be on the streets. Mom sends her a quid every month. It's not much but when you've a family our size you only need a little here and there.' He laughed. 'She probably gets more money from them than she did when Tommy was at work.'

'Aye, but she'd rather have her husband and son in her house and be a bit poorer,' said Joseph.

'Aye, of course she would!' said Kevin. 'I wasn't saying anything. Why d'you think I'm marching right now?'

'Alright, calm down, you nutters,' said Sean. 'This is supposed to be a peaceful march. We don't need you two brawling in the streets.'

The crowd began another round of *Men Behind the Wire* and they sang their lungs out.

> 'Armoured cars and tanks and guns
> Came to take away our sons
> But every man must stand behind
> The men behind the wire'

The song took them all the way down the Creggan and halfway down William Street. Their laughter faded when they reached the Rossville Street junction and saw people walking back from further along William street, scratched and bruised, soaked in purple dye.

Most of the march continued down Rossville Street, the boys included, starting down the final stretch. The lead lorry had vanished from view, but Joseph could hear the indistinct voice of a woman as it trailed up from Free Derry Corner. She must have been trying to organise the marchers, so it didn't get too messy. She obviously didn't know about the trouble down William Street.

'Did you hear what happened?' said a voice behind them. Joseph turned to see a man with wide eyes talking loudly to a woman next to him. He was breathing heavily.

'Back up William Street. People are saying that two guys have been shot.'

'So?' the woman said. 'People get shot here all the time. Rubber bullets are always flying.'

'No, real bullets,' said the man. 'They were shot with real bullets.'

'Aye, sure, and my dad's the Pope. Don't believe everything you hear. We're hardly the IRA.'

Joseph laughed. He didn't believe it either. Things were bad, sure, but they weren't so bad that people were shot dead. Even the Brits weren't that mad. Rubber bullets and water cannons were the usual thing, he'd heard, if a riot happened. And that was only in Belfast really. Derry was much calmer.

As they reached Glenfada Park, the march slowed. Across Rossville Street was a barricade made of rubble. People could pass down the sides of it, but marching was difficult.

And then, in a rush of surprise and terror, soldiers erupted from the flats and the park. An entire battalion charged onto Rossville Street and began firing. He'd heard how painful rubber bullets were and he didn't want to get hit, but he didn't panic. And then the crowd scattered, but he knew marchers to be tough and brazen. They should be fighting back. Instead they all ran.

'Shit, Joe! We need to get outta here!' Kevin yelled. Joseph couldn't move. Sean had already bolted, but Kevin was waiting for him. He watched as the crowd stampeded away in all directions; to the flats, to the park. Some tried getting past the barricade. People were climbing over it rather than going around to get out faster.

Three boys, not too much older than Joseph, were stood at the barricade. They were doing their best to help people round and over. Then one of them flew back, blood pouring onto his shirt. The other boys screamed. Kevin was still yelling. Joseph watched as the face of one of the boys disappeared into a red and black mess, before he collapsed, dead. Less than a second later, a bullet flew through the last boy's head, blood spattering on the barricade.

'Joe, we need to go now!' Kevin yelled, his voice tearing at his throat. Kevin grabbed him and pulled.

Joseph felt his body begin to shake. His eyes were wide, his brain a mess of thoughts and emotions that he couldn't process. He still couldn't move. He knew he had to, to get to safety. Away from the soldiers, away from the death.

Doggerland
MESOLITHIC
Gregory Leadbetter

This is the tide of the earth's tilting,
of years too long before, too far ahead
for thoughts tied to the daily sun,
the closed grip or gift of seasons – of utmost
memory, and beyond that, myth, animal-shapes
known to speech but never seen.

Today the past returns as water,
drowns the future with last summer's camp.
No rush for now, only the need for higher ground
and new words for that distant feeling
as they sat, warm and dry, looking down
over the blue plain, bereaved.

from *The Fetch* (Nine Arches Press, 2016)

Foraging

Serena Trowbridge

I know the hawthorn berry well. At first touch cool, smooth,
a worn patch like the tarnish on my grandmother's pendant,
touched daily, hourly with uncertain prayer for a husband's safe
return. Firm to the fingers until a squeeze explodes it like a
tiny scarlet bomb, the berry jagged crimson, white flesh creamy,
raw. I know the hawthorn berry intimately, archaeologically,
explicitly: exhumed from my mind with the weeping woman
whose sadness smelt of hawthorn.

The rosehip often disappoints. No scent of roses, after all, but
flaccid stink of old tomatoes, easily squashed when overripe. I
pick bags of them, ignoring thorns which tear at skin like pages
of a book, and simmer them in oil, a potion for the skin, a salve to
brew up in the dark (the kitchen lights have gone again) while
muttering incantations. A connection blossoms in the gloom,
    with
women in dark times who picked and washed and brewed –
    who knows
what they concocted in the kitchens of their minds?

I know the elderberry for its juices. After the foam of sickly
    blossom,
that sticky mass which smells of June-death, the berries form:
multitudinous, umbelliferous, the rich purple staining fingers
    as I pick,
strip, clean, boil them with sugar to submission. I heard that
    witches love

the elder – perhaps it is the juices they get drunk on, brewed up
    in a
cracked brown betty, offering cups to neighbours' children.
    Maybe it
saturates your stomach with a blackening wave of paralysing
    colour, a
nauseous, secret, inner stain of death.

The honeysuckle is the most obscure: a scarlet bead like drying
    blood,
tough, unripe. I'll thread them for my jewels, drape myself in
    cords of
rubies like a queen. I know little of their effects; approach with
    caution,
says the book. Perhaps they numb like hemlock, slowly, a
    creeping death-
dread voyaging the veins, turning you to stone, tangling in
    your body as
the tendrils of the plant entwine, casting a net across you to
    reclaim you
for the soil. A vigorous plant, its love is suffocating, demanding
your affection as it knits itself to bone.

I know the homely blackberry best of all. Sharp green globes
    bristling
with brown shabby whiskers, or rich flabby form when
    over-ripened,
watery with disappointment, scented with earth and mildew.
    Then the
perfect fruit: elusive, bound to be there, somewhere near the
    nettles,
inside that spiky hedge, hanging over the water's edge, full,
    firm. The

promised sweetness is a trap which sends me hurtling through
   a ditch
and down, whirlpools of darkness opening up below with the
   spicy scent
of Autumn – down, with that fatal blue-black bullet.

Next there is old yew: its fruit translucent, tempting, smooth
   and matte; a
waxy finish calls the fingers to it. The tree spells life and death:
   what wives
have been tempted to slip into the graveyard in the dusk, to
   pick, to squeeze the syrup, carefully secrete the bitter seed of
   venom in a husband's dinner?
In the shadow of the moon's eclipse the Druids looked for life
   here, in
death's garden. I have not dared to touch one yet, the berries
   taunting me
with rosy siren call to tempt doom and lick. I might mistake it
   for a rowan, hurl it careless in my basket.

I also know the mistletoe: how it loves the yew, and oak – a
   solstice
parasite, its power waning when the berries fall. It offers magic
   balms:
fertility, passion, a pilfered kiss – an entry to a twilit world,
   hallucinations,
whirling, dizzying, breathless dreams of wild stamping,
   shrieking pagan
dances, sleeping on the sacrificial stone, a life beyond the edge
   of human
sense. The berries make you ill, perhaps to death – but what a
   thrill! the

colour and the movement of the dead beckon me from the hill,
   the very
stones can hurl themselves towards the sky, and crash to earth
in fragments of a world.

Diced Beef

Danny Maguire

'Have you got everything?'

'Yes.'

'You're sure?' I picked up my rucksack and slung it over my shoulder. The duffle coat cushioned the pull of the straps.

'Yes,' said my husband. 'I've checked, checked again, and checked again.'

'All the papers?'

'That's what I meant when I said I have everything.' He closed our front door. 'Our identity cards, passports, permission papers.'

'Do you have the pictures?'

'Of course. Bubble-wrapped tight.'

'And you didn't pack any food, did you?' I asked. He rolled his eyes.

'How stupid do you think I am?'

I sighed. Travelling from one city to another was bad enough but travelling into the Capital brought the stress to a whole new level. Not only did we need all that, but if we were too low on the Origin Constituent System we wouldn't even get on the train. We were both lucky that none of our ancestors were on the wrong side of history.

We walked to the station. Cars were a privilege reserved for the Capital; the government weren't too fond of the idea of free movement. They liked to know where everyone was and when. We didn't have any other form of public transport other than the train. After a while, the weight of the bag made the straps feel like blades, cutting into my shoulders.

'Do you want to swap bags?'

'Your bag's just as heavy as mine,' I said.

'You look like you're in pain.'

'I am in pain.'

'I'm a man.' He flashed a grin.

I rolled my eyes. 'And I'm a weak woman?'

'You're really going to do this to me?'

'What? Call you out?' I slapped him lightly when his face went sour, the bag strap jolting my shoulder. 'I'm only joking.'

We walked on to the train station.

Sparks flew from the old, damaged brakes that screeched against the track as it pulled into the station. Guards in black uniforms stood on the platform, batons and handguns strapped to their belts. The platform was overloaded with people. Some were crushed up against the crumbling, rotting walls, while others stood on the edge, desperate to get onto the train.

It was full of people, inside and on top. The carriages were near bursting and the roof was crammed with those who couldn't fit down below. All sorts of people crowded together, keeping close to the centre. There were no smart-suited men with briefcases, only people like us. A sickly woman swaddled her baby close to her chest. An old man with a harsh burn on his faced watched her with sad eyes. Children sat and lay around the roof with parents, grandparents, aunties or uncles; any attempt to stand was quickly shut down with a shout. We all had to keep our heads low to avoid the overhead lines. Like us, the passengers were anxious. The country was dangerous, but the Capital was the riskiest city.

When we finally stopped, a two-way stampede ensued. Alighting passengers forced their way through the crowd of people who were fighting not only to get on the train, but to find a safe space to sit or stand.

The passengers were pressed tightly against each other as close to the centre as possible. The risk of falling from the roof was high. There were no barriers along the edge. The roof was only supposed to be walked on when the train was stationary but having passengers on the roof meant that fewer trains had to run, and less money had to be spent. No one would give up their seat for the elderly. You looked out for no one but yourself, but I couldn't help but watch other people and feel their suffering.

We watched as an old woman climbed up from amongst the chaos. She had lank greying hair spilling out from the inside of her hood. We grasped our bags between us, away from the wandering hands. She wore a vibrant, oversized red coat which caught the eye of many passengers. Even with it on we could see the contraband peeping through, giving her bulges in odd places. She had a cellophane bag of meat; beef, I imagined. It was a rare delicacy here. If you had some, you didn't waste it, but taking foods into the Capital came with the strictest of penalties. My husband saw it too and gave me a look. I glared at him and shook my head. He glared back. We argued without saying a word. In the end, silence fell between us and we ignored the old woman, who had been forced to sit with her legs hanging off the side. The train rattled on out of the station.

We left the grey, ugly building and the city altogether, and passed into the countryside. In the summer, it was beautifully green. The trees full of colour, the grass full of life, bringing joy and hope to this desolate land. It was autumn now. The trees half full of orange and brown leaves, the grass littered with the fallen ones. In the distance, above the Capital, grey clouds brewed, threatening a storm.

We arrived in the Capital in the early evening, rain soaking us through and drenching the roof. It was littered with hands of people trying to stop themselves from falling. As we passed through the West Station, the track turned off-course. It travelled along the river and took us past the magnificent statues of our previous Great Leaders. Behind the 20-feet-tall bronze idols, which gleamed despite the stormy sky, was a mural of the Mountain where our first Great Leader concocted the plan to rid us of the invaders, and the birthplace of his son. We all saluted the statues. If it weren't for the overhead cables, we would've stood.

We pulled into the Central Station. The storm had been and gone, leaving the tracks wet and slippery. The guards milled around the platform at this station too, weapons at their side. The old woman rose to her feet as it slowed. Fool. When the train stopped, it slid forward unexpectedly, and the woman stumbled. I nearly jumped from my space, as if to grab her before she fell.

She caught her balance, saving herself from certain death. Except her coat opened, and out fell the plastic bag. I could clearly see large pieces of diced meat, coating the inside with blood. The bag fell onto the platform at the feet of a guard. My stomach dropped. Our discretion was all for nothing. The woman's eyes widened as the guard looked up at her.

'You have the papers for this?' the guard called up. The woman took a deep breath, raising her head and pulling her shoulders back.

'Yes, yes, of course,' she said. 'They're inside my coat.'

'Give them to me,' he ordered.

'This is my stop. I can hand them to you on the platform.'

'Hurry up,' said the guard. 'The train is about to leave.'

Her face turned to steel and her breathing tensed. She'd be on her way to a Re-education Camp within the hour. At her age, she'd never get out.

'I'm an old woman. Could you help me down?'

The guard gave a deep sigh. Clearly, he didn't think he got paid enough for this. He gave her a nod and reached up a hand. The old woman took a firm grip of the guard's hand. She paused for a moment as the air emptied out of her body, before shooting her free hand up and tightly gripping the overhead line.

Her body became rigid as electricity coursed through it, burning her hand and stopping her heart. The smell of roasting meat and electricity filled the air. The woman's hand slipped from the overhead line, and she fell, crumpling onto the ground, two bodies left on the station's platform, as guards surged forward. Our train trundled on.

Be Here Now
Poppy Cartridge

INT. DR. SULLIVAN'S OFFICE -- AFTERNOON

The office is modern, almost excessively neat.

GIA (early 20s, poised, polished) and SEAN (27, subdued, dark circles under his eyes) sit as close as possible on the couch.

GIA'S HAND ON SEAN'S KNEE -- gripping tightly -- curved like a claw.

DR. SULLIVAN (late 50s, cautiously jovial, masking apprehension) skim-reads a well-annotated document on his desk.

> DR. SULLIVAN
> Do you frequently have trouble
> sleeping?

Sean observes the world outside the office -- congested roads, high rises -- life going on. Squinting from the bright sunlight streaming in.

> DR. SULLIVAN (CONT'D)
> I'll get the blinds.

He observes Sean discreetly.

Returns to his seat.

Arranges his pencils in a perfectly straight line.

Silence.

Sean turns his gaze towards him. Doesn't move at all -- almost held in place by Gia.

> SEAN
> Yes. I was taking sleeping pills

but--

He rubs his eyes, fidgets in the chair, as if
irritated.

Dr. Sullivan seems pleased -- there is the sense
that there has not been much response from Sean.

> DR. SULLIVAN
> And the pills... they didn't help
> at all? Alleviate anything?

> SEAN
> No.

> DR. SULLIVAN
> Can you pinpoint exactly when you
> started to have trouble sleeping?

He leans back in his chair in anticipation --
senses that he may get the answer he needs to
develop the discussion.

> SEAN
> No.

Dr. Sullivan shrinks. Knows that SEAN IS LYING.
Determined for an affirmation.

> DR. SULLIVAN
> Maybe we could talk a bit about
> your marriage?

Sean doesn't hide his reluctance.

> SEAN
> It started off well enough.

> GIA
> Yeah, they always do.
> (to Dr. Sullivan)
> Sean checked out a long time ago.

Sean shakes his head, defensive.

>   SEAN
>   I always tried, but--

Sean runs a hand through his hair -- almost
pulling it out.

Sean GETS UP, as if to leave.

Gia moves to the opposite end of the couch.

>   GIA
>   I can't listen to this.

>   DR. SULLIVAN
>   Okay, okay.

Attempting to defuse.

>   DR. SULLIVAN (CONT'D)
>   Sean, we're making progress--

>   GIA
>   How are we making progress?
>   Yet again he's avoiding
>   responsibility.

>   (to Sean)

>   Now sit down.

Sean SITS BACK DOWN.

>   DR. SULLIVAN
>   It's important to remember there
>   is no single reason why a session
>   is necessary.

Considering his words carefully.

>   DR. SULLIVAN (CONT'D)
>   Sometimes things such as emotional
>   stressors,or psychological trauma
>   can bring the issue to light.

LONG SILENCE.

A CAR HORN BEEPS for a few seconds.

CLOCK TICKS.

AIR CONDITIONING HUMS.

Sean speaks quietly, measured.

> SEAN
> I don't... want to talk about that
> sort of stuff.

Sean looks straight past Dr. Sullivan. Focuses on
the wall behind him.

> DR. SULLIVAN
> I understand it may be difficult
> for you, Sean, but in order to
> progress in these sessions we must
> assess the root of the problem.

> SEAN
> I can't talk about it.

> DR. SULLIVAN
> What do you think could be done
> to encourage you to address the
> issue?

SIMULTANEOUSLY: GIA SEEMS TO ALMOST SPRING TO LIFE
-- sighing impatiently, clinging to Sean's arm in
a PSEUDO-AFFECTIONATE GESTURE.

> GIA
> Jesus Christ, Seany. Of course you
> would be the victim in this. It
> always has to be about you.

She laughs sarcastically.

Dr. Sullivan and Gia's questions overlapping --
WORDS BECOMING GARBLED.

> GIA (CONT'D)
> Do you think that any of this is
> your fault, Sean?

Both Dr. Sullivan and Gia look at Sean, awaiting
his answers.

                    SEAN (TO DR. SULLIVAN)
          I can't talk about it because--

He stops abruptly.

Dr. Sullivan and Gia speaking simultaneously
again.

                    DR. SULLIVAN
          Yes?

                    GIA
          Go on. You'll only look fucking
          crazy.

Once again Sean focuses his attention on the view
of the BUSY ROAD outside the window.

CLOCK TICKS.

AIR CONDITIONING HUMS.

It seems as though Sean is going to remain silent,
and then--

                    SEAN
          I wish-- I wish we'd never stayed
          in that hotel.

                    GIA
          Remember, you requested the room
          with the balcony.

Sean holds his head in his hands -- words muffled.

                    SEAN
          She won't -- she won't let me talk
          about it.

He sounds tired, despondent.

Dr. Sullivan writing furiously, not looking up.

                    GIA
          Don't you dare blame me.

Dr. Sullivan looks over his page.

Realisation on his face as he processes Sean's words.

> DR. SULLIVAN
> Who is "she", Sean?

> SEAN
> Gia.

Dr. Sullivan's hand freezes above the page. Puts pen down.

> DR. SULLIVAN
> Gia?

> SEAN
> She always tells me it was my
> fault. But I did--

He looks directly at Dr. Sullivan.

> SEAN (CONT'D)
> I asked them to move us to a room
> with a balcony.

Dr. Sullivan turns over the paper on his desk -- reveals a NEWSPAPER CLIPPING, highlighted.

TRAGEDY AT BELMONT HOTEL AS WOMAN FALLS FROM BALCONY.

> SEAN (CONT'D)
> She's always here.

We SEE THE OFFICE FROM DR. SULLIVAN'S SIDE OF THE DESK.

He looks up slowly -- sees SEAN SITTING ALONE ON THE COUCH.

Leans in to his notes as if to write something, but pauses.

Silence.

> DR. SULLIVAN
> Is she here now?

Sean looks up. CATCHES HIS REFLECTION IN A MIRROR opposite the couch -- GIA BY HIS SIDE.

                    SEAN
          Oh, yes.

Dr. Sullivan scribbles furiously.

Sean looks down at his arm.

Red imprints of Gia's fingers in the flesh of his arm.

Sean speaks with a sad acceptance.

                    SEAN (CONT'D)
          She never left.

FADE OUT.

Toothbrush

Shulamit Ferber

It was a plastic wand-like object with hard white bristles on one end and pink grip lines halfway down. It was the first thing I added to his place. When we met, I enjoyed the smell of the Jägerbombs fizzling and dancing between our mouths in the Uber home. On another night, distracted by the electricity he held at the tips of his fingers, I let the chips we'd eaten at the end of our date cement into my molars. By morning, I'd wake to him laughing at me, reminding me of all the places where the chips were still sleeping between my teeth. I thought they'd be safe hidden from his ridicule. Did he actually care or was it just something I thought he cared about? Like my hairy legs? Or snail trail? I didn't realise how hairy I was until I met him. No, he promised me that was my choice.

But I still couldn't bring myself to give him one of the few things I had left. See, my thoughts had been taken over by the way his face creases when he smiles. My lunchtimes were no longer just me but spent in the sunlight with him; my best friend's favourite Starbucks drink was written down on his Notes in his phone. So, I dug my heels in, stomped on this imaginary, but badly needed, toothbrush.

Instead, I decided to put Smints in my overnight bag. I'd slip one in when he curled up into me. He'd fall asleep with my fingers crossed hopefully in his soft hair. But even then his lips would find mine on one of the many morning afters, and his tongue would leave furrier than it had ever been before. I'd tried fighting it. It was decided I needed to stop being disgusting and change my mind about getting a toothbrush. Although, in my final appeal, I did try to reason with him that we'd swapped quite a bit of saliva by this point so wasn't using his toothbrush the same thing? I thought so, but apparently not.

And then it was the first night with my toothbrush in his stained toothbrush holder. We'd put on our pyjamas and gone to his bathroom. He was stood at the mirror and I was sat on the toilet seat lid. And there we were just being. I was trying, pretending the brush brush brushing was enough to fill our new silence. My legs were crossed patiently and my fluffy socks were keeping my feet warm. But my knee was jumping, ready to spring next door and retrieve my phone from his room; ready to put my shoes back on and kick his door down. But none of this mattered, right? As long as my mouth was clean and my toothbrush was in his holder. Right?

As long as my shampoo, conditioner and, most importantly, my shaver were next to his in the shower. As long as we split groceries and eat all our meals together. Right? And never leave each other at parties. And never sleep in separate beds. Never be apart. Ever. That's what he wanted right?

But our silence during meal times became stifling: I found myself staring more at the lives of my friends on Instagram than his emerald eyes. What's wrong with me? Am I pushing him away or is he purposefully taking longer showers than usual? Come to think of it, he's only recently started reading before bed. Have we become domesticated too quickly?

It was a relief when I saw what he'd been up to. I was throwing out his junk mail and that's when I noticed them: in the bin, next to my ASOS delivery receipt, was all my toiletries. Taking the stairs two at a time, I couldn't help thinking that I'd just bought a new body lotion. To my relief, the tinny thwack of the bin lid ricocheted across the bathroom exposing its contents: the pink toothbrush. He'd done it.

As I stared at the mirror above the toothbrush holder, a huge toothy grin stretched to my eyes, my mouth slightly ajar from laughter: maybe we were going to make this work after all.

Foxglove
Derek Littlewood

In the woods, I missed my blue flower, but lit on
    a purple spire of foxglove, Zeiss-sharp,
in a shaft of sunlight. I see it twice, my left eye transforms
    itself into a pearl – clear proof of Novalis's cloudy words –
a sheen of violet haze, cataract of falling waters –
    Everything visible is connected to the invisible.
Cataract from Latin: *cataracta*, waterfall, portcullis, floodgate.
An opacity
    of the crystalline lens of the eye which will soon demand
the knife. In the brightness, a throb of pain,
all seen in slatted light – a jalousie.
    The beauty of blurred vision a ripe sour sight.

Odin-eyed towards the top of the spire
    Digitalis purpurea monstrosa,
a singular bowl-shaped cyclops flower, erupts as a genetic floral
surprise.
    Woodclearings murmur presences while trees come and
    go.
I slip my finger into the cool corolla
    to touch twin yellow nectaries
    waiting for the bees.
Odourless bells ringing
    each dappled like bacteria
in a Petri dish.
    Double foxglove, eyebright,
elusive fern-flower,

terminal peloria — a monster growth stops the spire with an overgrown
flourish. No foxglove tea or bitter leaf on buttered bread to race my heart.
Instead the thrill of a dark sublime.

Sekretas

Derek Littlewood

Woodchild delves in soil, then in the hallow
smooths sweet wrapper foils,

drops oak leaves, beech, a flash of yellow
buttercup, the smooth and hedgehogged

leaves of holly, all pinned together with spikes
of blackthorn. Last she slips over a shiver

of broken glass. Tamps the earth around
the edges with careful fingers:

at the bottom of her ice pool looms a garden.
Now she comes too close to you,

breathes in your ear – *Sekretas* –

The Edge

Courtney Hynes

FADE IN:

EXT. PERRAN SANDS HOLIDAY PARK, CORNWALL - DAY

An angry sea CRASHES against the cliffs. Static
caravans lined along the cliff edge.

INT. CARAVAN - DAY

DETECTIVE MASON STEELE (30s, a together man) sits
at the window with the view and watches MARTHA (an
elderly lady) move around the caravan.

SANDRA (Martha's chatty childhood friend) sits
opposite Steele. He continues to study Martha.

>   SANDRA
>   So you see, Sir, Martha here been
>   at home all evening alone when I
>   popped in to say g'night... Sir?
>   Sir Steele?

Steele finally looks at Sandra.

>   STEELE
>   Yes, Sandra, that's all
>   very helpful. Thank you for
>   volunteering to sit here with me.

>   SANDRA
>   Did ya get the part 'bout me
>   seein' Martha here's husband,
>   Roger, just up near t' cliffs
>   there?

She points out of the window and we see the cliff
edge.

> STEELE
> Yes. What time was that?

He holds a pen to a notepad.

> SANDRA
> Around nine o'clock, Sir. Just
> before he, ya kno'...

She motions to Martha with her tongue.

Steele pretends to take notes.

He notices Martha behind Sandra. She dusts the top
of a clean dresser with a dirty cloth.

A distraction.

> SANDRA
> Around nine o'clock it was, just
> before I made me way up t' here.

Steele continues to observe Martha's steps. She
moves sheepishly.

Beat.

> STEELE
> Martha?

Martha jumps lightly.

> STEELE (CONT'D)
> Were you with your husband
> yesterday evening at all, Martha?
> Before he went for a walk?

> SANDRA
> Oh, no. Ya see, Sir Steele, Roger
> always liked goin' a stroll on his
> own on the evenings.

> STEELE
> I'm sure Martha can answer on her
> own, Sandra.

                    SANDRA
                (quieter)
            She hasn't been well, Sir. I been
            looking after me Martha.

                    STEELE
            Yes, I've been told about the
            medication by an associate... you
            are taking your medication, aren't
            you, Martha?

Martha's eyes dart across the floor.

Beat.

Martha KNOCKS a glass from the dresser.

It SMASHES.

She picks up the pieces. Steele helps.

She picks up a large piece but drops it.

Martha moves quickly into the kitchen.

                    MARTHA
            Cup of tea will do the trick. We
            can all do with a good cup of tea.

She makes no eye contact with either party.

Steele observes the cramped kitchen.

An organised mess.

                    SANDRA
            Don't worry, Sir Steele, I'll get
            t' cleaning this up. Why don't ya
            sit back down

She nudges him to sit.

His eyes don't leave Martha's SHAKING hands as she
preps the tea.

He notices a TUBE OF PILLS on the windowsill.
Full.

                    STEELE
        Sandra, I think it's best you
        leave so I can speak alone with
        Martha.

Sandra pauses.

                    SANDRA
        I think Martha prefers me here,
        Sir.

Beat.

                    STEELE
        I won't ask again.

She takes a step. Stops.

                    SANDRA
        I'll always look after me Martha
        here, Sir Steele.

        A last glance at Martha.

                SANDRA (CONT'D)
        She's been a dear friend.

She leaves.

Beat.

Deathly silence.

Steele looks around the caravan. Pictures of
Martha and Roger are dotted around in small metal
frames.

A man's knit crew jumper lays neatly across the
arm of a fabric armchair.

An array of ties neatly hung across an open
wardrobe door.

There is a gap. ONE IS MISSING.

Steele holds his gaze at this gap.

He walks over to the window seat to peer at the
cliff edge.

                    STEELE
          Seems strange.

He remains at the window.

                    STEELE (CONT'D)
          An elderly man like your husband,
          to go out walking in a tie. And so
          late...

We hear Martha still in the kitchen, a teaspoon
CLINKING against a china mug.

                    MARTHA
          He always dressed smart.

Steele notices small specks of red on the
windowpane.

Blood.

                    STEELE
          Can you tell me where you were,
          Martha? Yesterday evening before
          your husband fell?

He moves to the kitchen doorway.

Eyes on Martha.

                    STEELE
          Nothing in regards to the
          incident?

Martha shakes her head.

                    STEELE (CONT'D)
          Or why you haven't been taking
          your medication?

Martha freezes.

She stops stirring the tea.

Steele approaches.

He stands close to her.

              STEELE (CONT'D)
        Or, Martha, you could just tell me
        why you killed your husband.

FADE OUT.

Toad Road
Lucy Greenwood

At a young age I never knew what I wanted to be when I grew up. I always found the question rather odd. Of course, who you are and what you are going to do as an occupation isn't usually a separate concept to those who are asking the question. My mother would mildly protest at my life choices by leaving the paper open at the jobs section, casually mention that Melissa, Hettie's girl, was getting married next year and that they had already put down the deposit.

My stomach had swollen to the size of a honeydew melon. I was asked countless times by my mother if there was any chance I could be pregnant, she wouldn't judge. I had spent the last two years travelling around Europe in an old Ford Transit van converted into a campervan, with a mattress set upon a crudely self-made wooden box frame and a camping gas double burner stove. It was simple, but the freedom it gave granted me the sense of home that others perhaps would find amongst bricks and mortar.

I had made small amounts of money for food and fuel by labouring on farms. Crop picking, mucking out and hedgerow laying. Evenings were filled with either gatherings of artists, musicians and storytellers or sometimes in complete solitude with only the sound of the waves, crickets and turning of pages in my book. I met many interesting people on my travels, but I guaranteed my mother, none were the potential father to the thing that made my stomach swell. In the hospital I had made it very clear that I was not to go under general anesthetic. The thought of another person putting me to sleep had always filled me with horror. Human error, probably my worst fear of all. I was administered a spinal block; I was awake throughout the procedure. I asked that they kept the screen down. Though I felt no pain I saw how the flesh of my stomach opened and parted with so much ease through the layers of flesh and fat. The latex-gloved surgeon rummaged around in my abdomen like looking for lost keys in a handbag. I heard the sucking and plunging sound from the mass that was pulled from my middle. Though the surgeon's face was masked, the widened look of horror in his eyes gave away his disgust. He recoiled, as in his hands was a ball of blood-soaked writhing toads.

Sleep came quite quickly after the surgery. A dream of rushing rivers through woodland, of horses neighing in terror, bucking and rutting as if trapped. I found myself buried in a giant ant hill with thousands of red ants swarming all over me, making my skin crawl. They filled my nostrils, my mouth, my eyes. I could hear the sound of their pincers snipping away at my flesh. As much as I scrambled and scratched at my body to get rid of them, another wave of ants would come, making light work of separating skin from bone like some time-lapsed footage of a decaying animal. I lurched out of my nightmare, gasping for breath as if still being drowned by ants. The nurse on the ward was doing her usual routine observations. She looked over at me with a sympathetic look, or was it a knowing look? Did she know what was removed from my belly? The harsh fluorescent strip lighting hurt my eyes. The smell of disinfectant permeated the air as I watched the streaks on the floor left by the mop slowly dry up. I kept my eyes fixed on the floor. My mother was sat by my bed. She was fidgeting and rustling the things that had gathered on my bedside. She had taken a magazine, flicked through the pages to the crossword and tapped her pen rhythmically as she tried to figure out 10 down, whilst I was trying to figure out what had happened to me. My post-surgery dream had made me think of a farm I had stayed at closer to home in the Welsh valleys. I had decided rather than go straight home from traveling, I'd ease myself in gently by spending a few days in Wales and then maybe a few in Devon or Cornwall.

I remember that I walked along a track through farmland. I placed my feet carefully over hoof-trodden mud and I stumbled over leaf-covered rocks. It was morning and the sun has started to rise in the east, so I knew I was walking south. Ivy-chocked trees lined the path I took. I had entered a wood covered in the colours of rust that crunched underfoot. I passed a small pond stagnant and still, reflecting the trees around it. Branches half submerged rose out of the water like hands grappling for something to hold on to.

The woodland separated a couple of hundred acres of farmland. A token to the fae and spirits my host had explained, as we sat around the fire on one of the first nights a group of us had arrived to do some work on their land. She was the daughter of the owner of the farm I had been working on. She was young but had an air of wisdom about her. Her hands looked older than her face, cracked and calloused, working hands. She explained the woodland had been left as it was, as it had always been, to appease the spirits of the place and all the faeries that lived there. We humans came along and reformed the land, used it for our own gain; we trimmed and tamed its wildness. She continued to tell us that it was no coincidence that you would see things move in your peripheral vision or see the shapes of spirits twisted in tree branches. Around the large fire in the courtyard she spun tales of magic, old folk magic. To her ancestors it was a way of living. They used magic for a bountiful crop, for commanding the animals they kept, for their own health and sometimes they used magic in matters of love and lust. This magic was not of fanciful potions or spells with almost unpronounceable words, but magic of the earth that used bones and stones, blood and spit. Hair, nails and piss filled bottles buried at crossroads. Once the stories had been shared and the fire turned in to embers of dancing light everyone turned in for the night.

The next morning, I had been asked to relay some hedge at the boundary of the woodland and the field. I carried a mallet, bow saw and secateurs in a black holdall. I was sure I'd find some hazel to cut for stakes to weave the hawthorn that grew between the wild and the tamed. The hedge ran along the path of a three-way crossroad made from the treaded path of a public right of way. I drew the blade of the saw across the stems of hawthorn. It was already heavy with blood-red berries and I wondered if we were going to have a bad winter. In amongst the thicket of haws I could see something in the bush. It was tied onto a branch. It appeared to be bones tied to string at regular intervals. To get a closer look at what I had found I took the secateurs and snipped at the string. As I grabbed it, I felt the unmistakable texture of hair, the string was made of hair. I could not tell if it was human or animal, the bones resembled that of a frog or toad.

I put the strange talisman in my pocket. Maybe someone at the farm knew what it could be. After dinner I presented my find to my host. I thought she would find it as fascinating as I did, her brow furrowed and squinted at me in confusion. 'Why did you take this from the wood'?

'I...I thought it was interesting, I wanted to find out more about it'. She looked at me wistfully.

'And you most certainly will, my dear'. She left without explaining any more.

A nightmare arrived. It cantered into my sleep with speed. I was still on the farm, mountains either side cast their ombre silhouettes against the watery light of the rising sun. I followed a moss-covered single track road that lead to the stables. As I entered the smell of fresh hay and horse muck filled my nose and made my eyes water. In the stables I could hear the systematic sound of shovelling. The shovel scraping along a concrete floor. I could see the defined muscles of his back all working independently of each other as he bent over his shovel as he worked. Slowly he turned around with his huge bulging eyes fixing me to the spot, unable to move. He strode over to me, his cold clammy hands everywhere. As I tried to block his advances another limb and more hands came from behind. I could no longer tell how many others could have been in the stable, I stayed as still could, as if perhaps I could just detach from the mauling of limbs and wait. Staring at the rafter beams of the stable the sunlight highlighted spiders' webs. I began to count them until I could feel no more. The bone and hair had still been in my back pocket. I had decided to look up what these items could possibly mean. I was inspired by my host's stories of magic, and she let me look at her collection of books in the library. A small room that smelt of years of burning sandalwood was covered wall to wall with ramshackle bookshelves stuffed with books on herbal remedies, bee keeping and other agricultural practices. One of the large bookshelves heaved with books on traditional witchcraft, Tarot and Astrology. I reached for a book of collected sources of folk magic. I flicked to the index and looked up toad.

Toad magic, it seemed, was used by stablemen to have better control over the horses in their care. Dead toads were buried in ant hills to rid them of flesh. The toad bones were considered magical. Not only was this magic used on horses, but also people. Women would use them in hope of attracting a man, though this magic also came with a warning. That a man's advances could become more than you had desired. In disturbing this toad bone, I had awoken an old magic and now I was facing the consequences.

I sat in my hospital bed, I could feel the stitches of my stomach pulling tight, itching as the skin was knitting back together. Toads and horses and limbs rolled around in my mind. It's hard to remember what was real and what haunted me in my sleep. The brain likes to fill in gaps when pieces of information are missing. The nurse came and handed my mother something wrapped in a blanket. My mother began to weep. The nurse gently told her that with time I would come round. I peered into the blanket that my mother's arms cradled. What am I going to do with a ball of toads?

Fortune
Amanda Smyth

Extract from a Novel in Progress

It took thirty-five days to clear away the forest on the north side of Chatterjee's estate, the patch where oil first came up and dribbled around the stick like a miracle. Twenty-two forest men and women from the Tattoo Gang came with axes, picks and saws and they hacked and chopped through hundreds of trees: mahogany, cedar, pine; dragged away their branches and some smaller trees were lifted onto carts and pulled by buffalo. Women cut and tore at the undergrowth, culled the knotted and tangled bush seething with bacchaac ants and termite nests big like heads, stuck to the pale immortelles. These wilder parts hadn't been touched for years. Eddie came upon an armadillo, a howler monkey and a quenk. Unafraid, the creatures squatted on rocks and stared at him.

'Look,' Eddie said, to the others. 'We have company.'

He clapped his hands and the animals scuttled away.

Tendrils hung like thick ropes, tangled and knotted; so much so it often took days to clear a few yards. The workers were paid according to the number of felled trees and by the amount of earth they'd shifted. Eddie assured Tito, although slower, it was cheaper than bulldozers and trucks. He reminded him of his own words. 'We're here to make money not spend it.' They worked from first light, stopped for lunch at 11am. There was rice, bread, beans, oranges. Sometimes Sita made cake or cut up fruits. They carried on until nightfall.

The sun was a bully, and Chatterjee said it was hot enough to die. The air was thick with mosquitoes and sand flies; then there were the jack spaniards. They caught in the hair of a 17 year old girl called Mercy; flew inside the tiny caves of her ears and when she opened her mouth to scream dived into her windpipe. Mercy was carried choking to the house where Chatterjee's wife soaked her head with vinegar and tipped aloe juice down her burning throat.

There were snakes: grass, anaconda, even mapipe, but the men and women were too quick for them. A swipe of the cutlass and their pointed heads were off—livers extracted and spread onto the worker's skin to stave off mosquitoes. Then Eddie himself found a 12 ft boa at the back of the outhouse curled up in the shade like a small child. He shot it first between the eyes, then decided to skin it without cutting. 'Look,' he said, holding up the mottled body, 'like taking a sock off a leg.' With this peeling and rolling came the birth of some ten small snakes, small and thin as bangles and half of them dead. 'You ever see anything like that?' he said, tipping the babies into a bucket. 'Delicious fried up like whitebait.'

Once the trees were gone, they started to level out the incline and the men dug hard into the dry earth and the women carried trays of this dug out earth on their heads to the designated place to support the damn, which Eddie said they'd need for overflow. Chatterjee couldn't imagine an overflow of any kind but Eddie told him it would come.

'As sure as I'm standing here, make no bones, the oil is right underneath me like a lake.'

Chatterjee admired Eddie's self belief. It was something he had never had; his nature was cautious, mistrustful.

Discarded tree trunks were split in four and once the ground was clear, laid down in a row like the dead, covered over with clay and gravel. And this is how the road into Chatterjee's estate was made.

It was hotter once the big trees were gone and the land became scorched and cracked like burnt skin. In fact, the whole place was singing and crackling with the heat of a furnace. But as Chatterjee said, at least it was dry, and it wouldn't be so for long. Rain go come.

Some days, Eddie worked alongside and helped where he could. He liked to take a spade and dig down deep, rub the damp earth in his hands, put it to his nose, lick it from his finger. He was no geologist but he had an idea of what to look for; and he was more than hopeful. Other days he left them to it and took the truck into San Fernando where Tito had leased an office above a shoe store on Coffee Street. There was a telephone, desk, kitchenette. Fernandes Wade Holdings, written on the sign outside the door. Just in case you forget who you're doing all this for. For the first time in his life Eddie felt like he was in charge. A far cry from his early days in Texas.

Eddie Wade saw his first well come in when he was 19 years old shaking peanuts in a field in Texas. The oil fountain shot up, and turned green and then gold, and he thought the earth was turning inside out. He had never seen anything more beautiful. In that moment, he knew what he would do with his life.

In Beaumont, as a young man, Eddie learned all he could from the boiler workers, the drillers, and mostly from boomers who swooped in, worked for a while, then moved on when they heard of somewhere better. He'd worked for a businessman who owned most of the town. Walter Well told him, You're going places, son. And by that I don't mean jail.

Eddie shared a shack with a Puerto Rican toolie. Walls were so thin, when a dust storm blew in the place rattled like a tin bucket. People got sick a lot. Beaumont water was soupy and tasted of frogs. It started with stomach cramps, high fever. If you caught 'the Beaumont's, you had to take a few days off.

Eddie was happy to stack pipe, feed the boilers, wash down the derrick, dig holes. For a time he was a roustabout, looking after the neatness of the field, picking up different broken rods, junk pipe. He dug ditches to manage waste water; he took care of repairs, made sure the tubes on boilers were swabbed. He looked after the steam engine, monitored the oil pumped form each well. When a whistle blew, you knew a well had come in. Everyone came to see and cheer. It was good manners to do so.

It was here in Beaumont that Eddie met Michael Callaghan. One night, after Eddie had just been paid, two men jumped him and stole his monthly earnings: $150. Callaghan saw the whole thing from his truck. He held up the men with a 45, marched them back to where Eddie was laying in the road, his face globbed up with blood. He told the bandits, 'The only talking I'll be doing is with my gun. So hand the damn money back to this poor sucker.'

A more experienced cable driller than Eddie, Callaghan was a bendy, scrawny man with red hair. A man for detail—Eddie might come with the big plan—Callaghan knew how to make it happen.

Some years ago, they'd followed a lead of Eddie's that took them five thousand miles south, along narrow trails into the dark heart of Santa Maria de Vitoria, El Salvador, where they found a skin of oily iridescence on the surface of Sau Francisco River. They set up camp. After two months of dry, sizzling weather, rains arrived early and suddenly. For ten days they were trapped in their camp, unable to move; sure they would die. They returned to Texas, poorer, thinner, their chests bubbling with phlegm.

Still determined, Eddie drove with Callaghan far across the rocky land, as far as Corsicana, as if they were the only men alive. South of the Cotton Belt railroad track they drilled and drilled. If a supply of hot artesian water came through, people came in hundreds believing it would cure all kinds of ailments. Old men with long beards got down on their stomachs and drank it.

When Eddie and Callaghan finally found oil, they were

scuppered by a crook now serving time for corruption in Auburn State prison.

Eventually, feeling defeated, Eddie left Texas and came back to Trinidad.

'It can do that to you; this oil business,' Callaghan told him. 'It's not a game for pussies.'

That day, the telephone line was faint and crackling. Eddie shouted into the mouthpiece.

'Kushi Estate—this is gonna be big, Callie. I mean real big. I can see the stuff bubbling.'

'Remember the preacher in Beaumont? He said the same thing; said he could see through the ground, and if you paid him fifty dollars, he'd hold his hands up to the sky like he was touching God.'

'He found that seepage up at the creek.'

'A fluke.'

Callaghan liked to tease.

'Those were the days of oil smellers and witches. Those days are done. You don't need special powers here.'

'The soil has sand? There must be clay, shale? What about gas? Is there a landing jetty? Without that we risk seawater damage. Where are the nearest facilities? Can we pump it out to a port? What about fresh water? You have a water supply? We can't do anything without water. What about this guy who owns the estate? He's not a crook?'

'Chatterjee? He's no crook. He's stubborn, but he's no crook.'

'It's not going to be like Salvador? Tell me that much.'

'Forget Salvador. Forget Beaumont. I know what you're thinking. But this is Trinidad. You hear me, Trinidad.'

Other men came from the villages: Tripe, Mr Long, Gelliseau, Horatio. Then Larry and Richard Gaskill were brought from Apex in Forest Reserve, after they jumped ship. He warned them, he couldn't pay Apex rates but he was glad to have them on board for as long as they could stay, which he figured wouldn't be so long. The oil business was a fickle business. The brothers were Scottish; their wives were waiting back home. Fair haired and loud, they liked to drink. Eddie told them there was no drinking on his watch. Especially once they started drilling. 'We'll need our wits about us.'

Gelliseau was strong, his arms ballooned with muscle, his back shaped in a V. He didn't say much but he knew about construction and had worked on the jetty at Le Brea. Mister Long was stringy and agile; he had laboured for years on a sugar estate. Long had eight children, from 2 years old up to 25. Then there was Horatio Sanchez. Eddie trusted Horatio at once; he had a steadiness about him, a sense of duty. When he smiled, his teeth had gaps between them like a picket fence. He lived in Claxton Bay with his mother; his father died in a cane fire when he was five. He'd worked on rigs in Barrackpore, Los Bajos, and for Venezuela Consolidated. He'd left Venezuela when Motelone Indians attacked the camp and fired a poisoned blow pipe arrow into the back of his friend who later died. Horatio was glad to be at Kushi, close to his mother.

More men from Danny Village would come, if and when Eddie needed them. He agreed a daily rate. For now, this was his team.

The Last Wolf in England
Serena Trowbridge

The last wolf in England
headed for the sea, skulking
in the meagre shadows
of the winter forest, lean
and grey. Its mate licked
a human pup at Ludgvan
and exhaled a lupine scream
    impaled on hunter's knife.

The last wolf in England
fled, freedom expired, moving
camouflaged at night, its arms
like branches and eyes like
moonshine, until it reached
the ocean. The last wolf
in England chose to leave
    the wooded land, paused

at the water's glittering edge
changed into a grey-scaled
fish, and slithered away.
The hunters got her in the end,
speared just off the coast
at Cadgwith, but her triumph
was they didn't know the magic
    that they slaughtered.

Sunday

David Roberts

That June it was hard for anyone to draw breath, so close was the heat. I was at his side when he fetched his last. Do you know what it is like? Have you ever witnessed such a thing? The agony of taking in air, pulling rocks up a hill, then the sigh that says do it again, again, but he's gone while you're wondering whether this will be the end. His hand clutched the bedpost tight, the knuckles twisted like a cashew tree.

For days he had been delirious. He kept begging forgiveness of his father. I could not tell whether it was his father he meant, or God. He spoke of them in the same way. The word 'reprobate' was new to me then and he used it very often of himself. Nor did I know he once had a brother. In his ramblings he would cry out to the boy not to run away for a soldier, or at the least to come back safe. 'Let there be one honest son in the family,' he groaned. One day he rose from his bed, naked, saying he was going to fetch meat from a place he called the shambles. I do not know what place that was but guessed he had been there long before – as a child perhaps, though I could not imagine him a child.

At the very last minute – it was just past three o'clock in the afternoon – he wanted water and asked for it to be brought from the spring by his stockade. 'No,' I said to him gently. 'It must be from our well here, at home.'

'Not – home,' he sighed.

'No. This is home'.

There was another word I knew I must say, a word I had always said, but somehow I could not, even though I knew it would reassure him. Now, as he lay before the doorway to the next world, it stuck in my throat. You may say I was ungrateful. But I think it was because I myself was standing, so to speak, at another doorway that I could not shape the word.

Master. When I first pronounced the word all those years ago, his face broke into what he said was his biggest smile since he lost his ship. As we walked back to the stockade, a goat slung over my shoulder, he made me say it over and over again. It was, he said, the most important word I could learn, second to *yes*; spoken together, he said, they were like a magic spell or a love potion. That evening, he would point to some task that needed doing, and with a glint in his eye he would urge me to repeat it. And *yes master* I would say, and he would laugh loud and rub his hands with delight. Then he showed me my bed outside the stockade wall.

But when the boy Marco put his head round the door and asked if the master was dead, the word came to me once more, riding upon a great wave.

'I am the master now,' I said.

Some were shocked when it was revealed he had left his plantation to me. Others did not believe me until I showed them the will and the deeds made over to me. I resolved to be a master in his image: kindly, firm, and with a constant devotion to the Lord's purpose. The slaves were to have time for prayer and song as well as labour. If they worked hard they would be cared for even unto death; if they neglected their tasks and fell into idleness, they would be whipped or cast out. It was as he had taught me.

And so I settled into the way of a plantation owner, carrying on my master's work in good spirits and the name of the Lord. My heart surged as I rose in the morning and heard the slaves going about their work, in full song. I admired even more the strength of my master's teaching. The plantation thrived; I grew rich beyond imagination. Although I missed my master, I could not remember a time when I had been happier.

Waking early one morning last November, I began to look for *The Pilgrim's Progress* among my master's books – *my* books, I should say. I had begun to think of myself as a pilgrim in this world, and my plantation as the kind of godly paradise every Christian seeks. I found the book, pulled it from the shelf and was about to turn away to sit and read when I saw another behind it, flat against the wall, as though it had slipped there, by accident or design.

I have no doubt you know my late master's celebrated work, *The Life and Adventures of Robinson Crusoe*. There are scandalous rumours that it is really the work of some London hack called Dufour, or Deffand, or some such, but I know otherwise. In it, I hear my master's voice calling to me, clear and true. We often spoke of the work, lingering long into the evening with his tale of how he rescued me from the cannibals who brought me to the isle. How I joyed to hear him recite the passage where I severed the head of my savage enemy and presented it to my master's feet! How I thrilled to hear of his great ingenuity in surviving so long upon the isle!

Now, if you know that story, you will recall there are episodes in it drawn from the day book (let us call it a diary) my late master kept in his solitude. Without it, he said, he would have lost all sense of time; his wits would have been blown to the corners of the isle and beyond, he always said, had he not marked every day with the passing of the sun and moon and the cries of the birds in the trees. I always wondered where that diary might be. When I questioned him, he said it had been lost in the commotion when the English ship came and rescued him (rescued *us*, I corrected him).

I considered the matter a while. It made me uneasy a little to think so, but eventually I said it.

'So master, when you wrote that work of your life and travels, you were only remembering what was true?'

'Ay, Friday,' says he. 'Such it is when you write the book of your life. There is only memory. Nothing else'.

'So master,' I continued, 'when you wrote out in your cele-brated *Life and Adventures of Robinson Crusoe* those parts of your diary, you could not be sure what was in it?'

'No, Friday.'

'Is that not –'

'No, Friday. It is not, if that is what you mean, cheating. It is memory. It is how these things are written'.

'But your diary, master – would it not have helped? Memory is like a firefly dancing in the light. Put out the light and it is gone.'

This was one of the few occasions when I remember my master becoming angry with me.

'Memory is enough,' he replied, reddening. 'There was no call for any diary. The diary is lost'.

At the time I wondered whether there was something else about this diary that should concern me, but I put it out of my mind. Until that morning, that is – the morning when I pulled aside *The Pilgrim's Progress* and found it, flat against the back of the shelf. My master must have had it newly bound. It was good calf, dusty from neglect but pliable in the heat. The pages crack-led. When I flicked through, paper shards fell to the floor, so I shut it up and kept it close. For all its leather finery, it seemed as though it might turn to sand. I would have to work fast if I was to read it.

So I set it down on my late master's great desk and began to read. The writing was jagged, as though he had begun in the midst of the great storm that brought him to the island. No doubt his hand trembled from the shock (you can see how I felt for him as I read). He wrote of the great wave that carried him ashore, of his trips back to the ship to recover tools and weapons; of the stockade he made to keep wild animals out, of his spreading grain in the ground by accident and seeing it grow, to his delight. He wrote of the young goats he reared, and the great bird he shot, and the way his flintlock echoed round the whole isle. Nor did he stint in hiding his despair or recording his appeals to God to release him from his torment. I could not forbear shedding tears as I read: everything was as you find it in *The Life and Adventures of Robinson Crusoe*.But my tears dried when I found there was more.

He had been on the isle ten years, by the diary's reckoning, when his crop failed and his goats sickened. The diary says he endured days without food. There were no fish he could catch and the powder for his flintlock was used up. Sword and dagger alone could save him. But how to use them? On what? They were no more use than the English money he had taken from the ship. All the knives in the world would not catch him a fish or a plump bird to eat. One entry, carrying the date of 12 February 1716, says he thought of hanging himself, or throwing himself from a cliff for sheer hunger.

Then the boat arrived. They were men of my tribe. Their craft beached in the western cove of the isle and they struck camp on the sand. He says he watched them, deploring their savage rites, their lighting of fires, and observing how they were preparing a prisoner for their banquet. But the man fought back. He ran from them, up into a thicket, so they lost him, setting up a great hulloo and fighting birds from the trees. The diary records how my master summoned the strength to take up his sword and make haste towards the cove in hopes to intercept the fugitive.

This was very strange to me. At first I thought he must be writing of my own deliverance, so I checked ahead in the diary through many months and years, hoping I might not find myself in the later parts of his story. I was disappointed. There I was, three years later almost to the day; rescued from a brutal death and taken to the stockade. Another, it seemed, had once filled my place.

I turned back to the diary to read of this first man on the run. My master wrote how he stopped him as he ran from the cove, his sword to the fellow's heart. The man's eyes were wild and his chest heaving but he gave in, putting his head to the ground before master's feet. My master took him up, said gentle words to him and led him back to the stockade where, because it was the Lord's day, he named him Sunday. Then, craving forgiveness of his fathers on earth and in heaven, he struck off the man's head and began to hew his limbs for roasting at the fire. According to the diary, the flesh tasted sour, like goat.

Pressing the calf covers hard between my hands, I ground the pages into dust and blew them across the desk. If he had been there, drawing out his last breath, I would have blown them down his throat. Just then, a breeze caught the dust and it billowed up. A chill like his spirit passed over me. Below, as the sun rose, the slaves started up their song. *Lord set me free,* they sang; *Lord set me free.*

Waiting for Lauren
Olivia Hodgson

Spilt branches creak for no owl,
but opiate dealing: the call
and recess of our night mimicked
by teenage girls and a rooftop siren's song

when at just the right doorway or two,
no moment more, we catch her –

between the curves of an hourglass
she wilts to life
under sodium-yellow rays,
from her leaf-soaked feet to her smoke-clung hair.

Notes on Contributors

Suna Afshan
Suna Afshan is a reticent writer of both prose and poetry and is reading for an MA in Creative Writing. In the summer of 2018, the School of English awarded her with the Mercian Prize for a collection of poetry. She is co-founder and editor at *Poetry Birmingham* which will release its maiden publication in the autumn of 2019.

Ravenna Allcott
Ravenna Allcott, age 20, is currently studying English and Creative Writing and is in her first year at BCU. Her writing surrounds dysfunctional domestic spheres and she loves creating characters who are 'rough around the edges'. Ravenna is in the midst of writing her first novel.

Poppy Cartridge
Poppy Cartridge is an undergraduate student, currently studying for a BA (Hons) in English Literature. She is particularly interested in the transgressive genre, and also enjoys Gothic literature.

Melanie Dillon
Melanie is in her first year of a part-time MA in Creative Writing. She is an avid reader, especially of children's literature. After years of telling herself stories in her head, she is now trying to get some of them down on paper.

Adrian B. Earle

Adrian B. Earle is a poet, playwright and storyteller; host and producer of the Verse First Poetry Podcast, an MA Creative writer and a spoken word poet who performs under the name Think/Write/Fly. He is a 2019 Hippodrome Young Poet and Publishing Manager at *Poetry Birmingham*. His debut pamphlet, *5000 HURTS*, will be published in October 2019 by Burning Eye Books.

Shulamit Ferber

Shulamit Ferber is a second year BA English student. While at university, she discovered a passion for creative writing, developing her skills and creativity through different forms of writing. Using her knowledge of short stories and audio dramas, she plans to extend her abilities to write for film.

Chris Fewings

Chris Fewings writes poetry compulsively and is learning to write fiction. He also facilitates creative writing groups and recites dead poets at open mics. A creative non-fiction pamphlet ('Birmingham Flows: reimagining city, countryside and self') arose out of his love for Birmingham's greenways, which follow its numerous streams and canals.

Lucy Greenwood

Lucy Greenwood studies English Literature and has been writing for four years. She enjoys blending the natural with the supernatural and hopes her writing is thought-provoking and entertaining. Lucy has ambitions to publish an anthology of short stories and poems inspired by folk magic.

Olivia Hodgson

Olivia Hodgson was born in 1995 and raised in Birmingham. In 2016, she won Birmingham City University's Mercian Prize for Poetry. She is currently studying for the MA in Creative Writing and is Co-Founder and Editor at *Poetry Birmingham*.

Courtney Hynes

Courtney Hynes is in her final year of English and Creative Writing and enjoys putting her skills to craft, particularly to write screenplays. She is currently working on a short screenplay which she hopes to film over the summer, as well as writing a fantasy novel for her last creative writing modules.

Portland Jones

Portland Jones is a pagan, aromatherapist, morris dancer, jewellery maker and drummer who has worked with the homeless of Birmingham. Portland is rebirthing her life, exploring her brave new world with writing to push back at trauma. Her latest venture is Witch Lit with a short story appearing in an anthology due at Summer Solstice.

Gregory Leadbetter

Gregory Leadbetter's poetry collections include *The Fetch* (Nine Arches Press, 2016) and the pamphlet *The Body in the Well* (HappenStance, 2007). His book *Coleridge and the Daemonic Imagination* (Palgrave Macmillan, 2011) won the University English Book Prize 2012. He is Director of both the MA in Creative Writing and the Institute of Creative and Critical Writing at Birmingham City University, where he is Reader in Literature and Creative Writing.

Derek Littlewood

Derek Littlewood lives in Worcestershire with Caroline and their two teenage children. He teaches writing poetry and literature at Birmingham City University. He has a poem in the Emma Press anthology *Second Place Rosette*: *Poems about Britain* (2018). You can see more of his work at www.dereklittlewood. com

Danny Maguire

Danny Maguire is a third year undergraduate of English. He is an aspiring author and screenwriter who enjoys writing fantasy and science fiction. He had a fantasy short story featured in the 2017 anthology *Timelines* and is hoping to start his MA in Creative Writing in September.

Kristof B. Marton

Kristóf B. Márton became fascinated with movie-making as an actor in his native Hungary and is now committed to screenwriting, having moved to the UK to study. His short screenplay 'Borderlands' captures a rapidly-disappearing Central European ambiance, from the perspective of a train driver on his final journey before retirement.

Charlotte McCormac

When Charlotte isn't blogging or writing technical marketing content, she's writing poetry and psychological fiction, often with magical elements. She is a student on the Creative Writing MA and has been published and shortlisted in a variety of magazines, journals and anthologies.

Max Mulgrew

Max Mulgrew is a Brummie who remembers when Austin made cars at Longbridge and Villa won the European Cup. He had various jobs before being indentured as a trainee journalist. He has worked on newspapers, in radio and television and online. Max is on the MA Creative Writing programme.

David Roberts

David Roberts is Professor of English at BCU. His most recent book, a biography of George Farquhar, was described in *The Irish Times* last year as 'wonderfully readable and meticulously researched'. Next up are a history of the Birmingham Hippodrome and a new edition of William Congreve's play, *The Way of the World*.

Naush Sabah

Naush Sabah works as a freelance writer and editor, whilst completing an MA in Creative Writing. Her short play, *Coins*, was produced at The Rep as part of the 2019 Write Away programme for playwrights. Her graphic novel, *Threads*, is currently in development with *Burnt Roti*. She is Assistant Editor at *Short Fiction Journal* and Co-Founder and Editor at *Poetry Birmingham*.

Amanda Smyth

Amanda Smyth is Irish Trinidadian. Her first novel *Black Rock* won the Prix du Premier Roman Etranger, was shortlisted for NAACP award, McKitterick Prize, and selected as an Oprah Winfrey Summer Read. Her short stories have appeared in *New Writing, London Magazine, The Times Literary Supplement* and broadcast on BBC Radio 4. Work on her third novel has been supported by Arts Council England.

Abbie Thay

Abbie Thay is an undergraduate student currently studying BA (Hons) English Literature. The dream of teaching English is taking Abbie across the globe. With a backpack bigger than her, she is ready to take her infectious personality into the classrooms of Thailand in September.

Serena Trowbridge

Serena Trowbridge reads a lot of poetry but has only recently started (admitting to) writing it. She lives in Worcestershire where she does a lot of walking and cloud-watching, and in her spare time, she is a lecturer in English Literature at Birmingham City University.

Rebecca Wright

Rebecca Wright is an undergraduate student, currently studying for a BA (Hons) in English and Creative Writing. She is an aspiring author, and wishes to branch out into children's literature in the future. In the meantime, her aim is to become a teacher, and she hopes to inspire future generations to pick up a pen and write. Her work can be found at https://rebeccawright1.wixsite.com/rebeccawrites